$\mathcal{G}$ET ALL THIS $\mathcal{F}$REE

WITH JUST ONE PROOF OF PURCHASE:

$50 VALUE

◆ **Hotel Discounts** up to 60% at home and abroad ◆ **Travel Service -** Guaranteed lowest published airfares plus 5% cash back on tickets ◆ **$25 Travel Voucher** ◆ **Sensuous Petite Parfumerie** collection ◆ **Insider Tips Letter** with sneak previews of upcoming books

$\mathcal{Y}$ou'll get a FREE personal card, too. It's your passport to all these benefits—and to even more great gifts & benefits to come!

There's no club to join. No purchase commitment. No obligation.

SR-PP5A

Enrollment Form

☐ *Yes!* I WANT TO BE A *Privileged Woman*.
Enclosed is one *PAGES & PRIVILEGES*™ Proof of
Purchase from any Harlequin or Silhouette book currently for
sale in stores (Proofs of Purchase are found on the back pages
of books) and the store cash register receipt. Please enroll me
in *PAGES & PRIVILEGES*™. Send my Welcome Kit and FREE
Gifts – and activate my FREE benefits – immediately.

More great gifts and benefits to come.

NAME (please print)

ADDRESS   APT. NO

CITY   STATE   ZIP/POSTAL CODE

PROOF OF PURCHASE
ONLY

**NO CLUB!
NO COMMITMENT!**
*Just one purchase brings
you great Free Gifts and
Benefits!*

Please allow 6-8 weeks for delivery. Quantities are limited. We reserve the right to
substitute items. Enroll before October 31, 1995 and receive one full year of benefits.

Name of store where this book was purchased_____

Date of purchase_____

Type of store:

☐ Bookstore   ☐ Supermarket   ☐ Drugstore
☐ Dept. or discount store (e.g. K-Mart or Walmart)
☐ Other (specify)_____

Pages
& Privileges™

Which Harlequin or Silhouette series do you usually read?

_____

Complete and mail with one Proof of Purchase and store receipt to:
U.S.: *PAGES & PRIVILEGES*™, P.O. Box 1960, Danbury, CT 06813-1960
Canada: *PAGES & PRIVILEGES*™, 49-6A The Donway West, P.O. 813,
North York, ON M3C 2E8

SR-PP5B

▶ DETACH HERE AND MAIL TODAY! ▶

"I want to marry you, Gloria."

The sincerity she read in his eyes stunned her.
"But—but—"

"You've got courage," he said, and she heard the
admiration and pride in his voice.

"That's no reason to marry someone!"

"No. But it's a reason you might take a chance on
me."

"Take a *chance* on you? What do you know about
me except that I teach etiquette and protocol for a
living?"

"I know you're a real lady."

She swallowed hard.... The most eligible man in
Tidewater had just asked her to marry him.

For all the wrong reasons.

Dear Reader,

This month, take a walk down the aisle with five couples who find that a MAKE-BELIEVE MARRIAGE can lead to love that lasts a lifetime!

Beloved author Diana Palmer introduces a new LONG, TALL TEXAN in *Coltrain's Proposal*. Jeb Coltrain aimed to ambush Louise Blakely. Her father had betrayed him, and tricking Louise into a fake engagement seemed like the perfect revenge. Until he found himself wishing his pretend proposal would lead to a real marriage.

In Anne Peters's *Green Card Wife*, Silka Olsen agrees to marry Ted Carstairs—in name only, of course. Silka gets her green card, Ted gets a substantial fee and everyone is happy. Until Silka starts having thoughts about Ted that aren't so practical! This is the first book in Anne's FIRST COMES MARRIAGE miniseries.

In *The Groom Maker* by Debut author Lisa Kaye Laurel, Rachel Browning has a talent for making grooms out of unsuspecting bachelors. Yet, *she's* never a bride. When Trent Colton claims he's immune to matrimony, Rachel does her best to make him her own Mr. Right.

You'll also be sure to find more love and laughter in *Dream Bride* by Terri Lindsey and *Almost A Husband* by Carol Grace.

And don't miss the latest FABULOUS FATHER, Karen Rose Smith's *Always Daddy*. We hope you enjoy this month's selections and all the great books to come.

Happy Reading!

Anne Canadeo
Senior Editor, Silhouette Romance

Please address questions and book requests to:
Silhouette Reader Service
U.S.: 3010 Walden Ave., P.O. Box 1325, Buffalo, NY 14269
Canadian: P.O. Box 609, Fort Erie, Ont. L2A 5X3

DREAM BRIDE

Terri Lindsey

Published by Silhouette Books

America's Publisher of Contemporary Romance

For Irene Manning,
who played Red-Light, Green-Light with me, a glass of milk and
Engineer Bill; who pulled cactus spines from my backside in the
glow of a trailer's kitchen light; who walked with me in the dusk
at Lake Isabella so we could see the bats and who continues to
make my life fuller and richer through her love.
Thank you, Nana

 SILHOUETTE BOOKS

ISBN 0-373-19106-5

DREAM BRIDE

Copyright © 1995 by Terri Lynn Wilhelm

Books by Terri Lindsey

TERRI LINDSEY's

experiences as a stockbroker taught her to expect the unexpected. "Like the time an angel-faced little grandmother came in," she recounts, "and announced she wanted to take advantage of a hot stock tip she'd received from a fellow poker player."

The one thing in Terri's life that was never unexpected, however, was that she would be a writer. As an adolescent she wrote for the entertainment of her family and friends. Today she writes for those who believe in that special bond between a man and a woman.

Terri lives with her husband and two dogs by a lake in Florida.

LUKE CAHILL'S DREAM BRIDE SCORE SHEET

Candidate: Gloria Hamilton   **Age:** 28

Occupation: Etiquette Consultant

Marital Status: Divorced

****

Check where applicable to candidate and award appropriate points.

✔	She conducts herself perfectly in any situation.	15 pts.
✔	She's an excellent hostess.	20 pts.
✔	She loves and wants children.	25 pts.
✔	She doesn't look, speak or act like a bimbo!	40 pts.

BONUS 10 points: ✔ She's a great kisser.

Total Points: __110__

(Note: If candidate scores higher than 100—
MARRY HER!)

Chapter One

There she was again.

Luke Cahill slowed his stride up the entrance walk to the Grimble Building.

He'd first seen his beautiful mystery woman two days ago. Since then, Luke had enjoyed walking behind her. The view brightened each morning considerably.

She was tall for a woman, maybe five-nine, five-ten, which, compared to Luke's own six feet four inches, was still quite short. Yet intriguingly compatible.

Her hair, pulled back as usual into a Grace Kelly kind of twist, was as dark and lustrous as one of his mother's sable coats. That meant her eyes might be green. Or blue. Or maybe brown.

But he knew for a fact she had to have the best-looking little fanny in Tidewater. No, make that Texas. Maybe even the whole country. It was high, and lush, and pert. Voluptuous. The perfect size for a man's hands. And with every step of those high-heel-clad feet, her long, slim, shapely legs set that delectable derriere into time-honored motion. In the straight skirt she was wearing, her feminine sway presented him a galvanizing vision.

He followed her into the lobby of the four-story Victorian his family's company had bought and renovated last year. Now his division of Cahill Companies—Texas Gulf Properties, Inc.—occupied the entire fourth floor.

They blended into a small crowd, and the black-veined marble floors and molded plaster walls echoed the constant murmur of multiple, low-voiced conversations.

Luke dodged the fronds of a tall potted palm as he entered the modern elevator that had been given doors covered with ornate, gold-painted metalwork and an interior lined with polished mahogany and thick, crimson carpet to keep it in the spirit of the nineteenth-century building.

The elevator was crowded and Luke stood directly in back of his mystery woman. They were so close, so very close.

He stared up at the ceiling, at the numbers indicating the floors, trying to recall his schedule for this morning.

The elevator stopped and the doors slid open. Several people exited onto the second floor, leaving more room for the few remaining passengers. Luke breathed a little easier and moved back, away from her. It was so damned warm in here. The doors closed and the elevator continued its ascent.

At the third-floor stop, everyone else poured out of the elevator, scattering to their offices.

To his astonishment, *she* returned, stepping around the edge of the elevator, back into sight. With a quick sweep of her hand, she stabbed the Stop button and turned to face him.

Eyes the color of sherry flashed in an oval face as fair as pearls. Bright color flagged high, elegant cheekbones and a generous mouth pressed into as tight a line as those full lips could ever manage.

"I've tolerated your disgusting behavior long enough," she snapped. "No more. The ogle stops here."

Shocked at being confronted, mortified at being caught, Luke felt heat rise up his neck. He cleared his throat, but she continued.

"If you don't stop harassing me, I'll report you to management."

His eyebrows drew down in confusion. "Who?"

"Management—the people who own and operate this building." Her lovely eyes narrowed. "Texas Gulf Properties."

"I see."

"Ha! That got your attention, didn't it? Well, if I so much as catch you peeking at my, er, my—" her color heightened "—posterior again, I'll take the matter up with them. I'm a respectable tenant who pays her rent on time. They'll listen to me."

Luke cleared his throat once more. "You're right, of course. I'm guilty. I have been looking at your...at you. I realize it's not very gentlemanly of me." *But you have a particularly delectable derriere.* "Please accept my apologies."

She looked slightly mollified. "Well." She straightened her shoulders.

Luke's discerning eye immediately detected the high, womanly curve of magnificent breasts under the camouflage of her short red jacket.

Instantly, he caught his mistake. Too late. She'd already followed the direction of his glance.

She leveled a look at him that would have frozen the Sahara Desert. Contempt saturated her voice. "Swine."

She smashed the Stop button and turned sharply on her heel. The doors rolled closed. Before Luke could reach the Door Open control, the engines were whining and the elevator had started moving up.

He glared at the closed doors and spat an especially vile oath. Any other time, the damned thing seemed to move as slowly as molasses in a Yankee winter. He swore again. Well, he'd have to go down and apologize to her, though he wasn't sure how inclined she'd be to accept his apology. First he had to find out what office she worked in.

Gloria Hamilton strode down the hall toward her office, fuming. Of all the nerve! Of all the absolute, unmitigated gall! She should have known he wouldn't have the decency to be ashamed. But to offer her a patently false apology and then flaunt it by looking at her bosom—what a creep!

She would have understood if he'd ogled her—briefly—just one morning. After all, she knew that by male standards she had an exceptionally nice bottom. Three days, however, was unforgivable. The guy probably had some kind of unhealthy fixation. Well, *she* wanted nothing to do with his problem. Tomorrow she'd wear a full skirt.

Gloria frowned. While she'd threatened to take the matter to Texas Gulf Properties, she doubted they could do anything to prevent him from looking at her. That's all he'd done, really. But that was too much. She was fed up with it.

If he continued to follow her, she'd go to Texas Gulf Properties, directly to the person in charge, and hope it would be enough to take care of that fanny fancier.

She liked her business's new location and hoped that her words in the elevator were all that was really needed. The architecture of the Grimble Building appealed to her traditional tastes, as did its location on Jetty Avenue—the avenue lined with Victorian structures containing offices, shops and restaurants. It was worth the moving costs and the additional rent to have her etiquette-and-protocol consulting business relocated here. Early on, she'd discovered the advantage of offering elegant ambience when dealing with upwardly mobile, often nervous, businesspeople. Now she could also add a smart address, a wise move that she expected to pay off handsomely. While she had sufficient enrollment to keep her busy now, she worked toward the day when there would be a waiting list for her services.

Reaching into her purse for her keys, she paused to admire the tasteful brass plaque next to the dark wood-veneered, brass-trimmed security door of her office.

Hamilton Consulting, Inc.

Not bad for a woman who, three years ago, had stumbled shell-shocked from her divorce attorney's office, impoverished and possessing no discernible job skills. Gloria restrained herself from breathing on the plaque and giving it an enthusiastic buffing with the raw silk sleeve of her jacket. She smiled. What would her students think? Her smile grew into a full-fledged grin. Actually, her students would probably understand. Most of them were business-people moving into new social situations, sometimes pre-paring to do business in foreign countries. Many had pulled themselves up to their present level of success by their own bootstraps; some came from disadvantaged backgrounds. Yes, she thought, they would understand.

She unlocked the door and stepped into a gracious wait-ing area furnished with a plush sofa and comfortable chairs, potted ferns and an Oriental carpet. All but the ferns had been purchased at various secondhand shops in Houston and Tidewater. Two of the chairs she'd upholstered herself. She knew the room looked inviting yet possessed an air of dignity, and no one but she realized the furnishings had not been purchased new from fine stores.

Alice Brackenbury, Gloria's secretary, swept into the of-fice. As usual, she wore her gray-and-wren-brown hair braided in a neat coronet. Today her squarish frame was clad in a blue dress and jacket trimmed with enough gold braid to draw a salute. She'd foregone her favored sensible shoes to wear black walking pumps.

"Good morning," Alice sang brightly, her words En-glish accented. She went to her desk and deposited her purse in the bottom drawer.

Gloria smiled fondly. Alice had come to the Hamiltons as a housekeeper when Gloria's father had been briefly posted to the U.S. embassy in London. Over the many years that followed, through relocations to remote embassies in un-stable countries, the down-to-earth Englishwoman had grown to be part of the family. She'd been with them through the death of Gloria's mother and through the end of Gloria's marriage. For years, Gloria had cherished a hope that her father and Alice would fall in love and marry. That wish had died when her diplomat father had wed a woman "more appropriate to his station and more beneficial to his career." Her father's new wife had immediately set about trying to drive off the housekeeper. Which had left Alice free to accept Gloria's offer of employment three years ago.

"Good morning, Alice. You're awfully cheerful this morning. Looking pretty spiffy, too. What's the occasion?"

"Oh, well," Alice said as she headed down the short hall to the nook where they kept the coffeemaker, the electric teakettle and the supplies for both beverages. She set about making their morning tea. "Vern is going to take me someplace special for lunch. He won't tell me where. A surprise, he says. Someplace nice."

Gloria had met Alice's suitor and liked him. Vern operated heavy machinery for a living and had the soul of a poet, but most important to Gloria was that he treated Alice like a queen.

"That's what you need, luv," Alice continued. "A nice beau. A big, strong, sexy man who can show you a good time and make you happy."

Gloria laughed. "Like Vern, for instance?"

Alice grinned over her shoulder. "Precisely, my dear. Every deserving woman should have a man like my Vern."

An image flashed into Gloria's mind. A Houston, twentieth-floor office late at night, illuminated only by the desk lamp. The sound of harsh, rapid breathing and an impassioned feminine voice pleading for more, *more.* Her husband hunched and bucking between the spread thighs of his writhing, naked secretary.

Gloria shook her head, wishing she could forget the horrible scene that had greeted her that night—that last night—when she'd gone to surprise her husband, who had claimed to be working late again. The Chinese takeout she'd brought to share with him had gone uneaten. For all she knew, the bag could still be sitting outside his office door where she'd dropped it.

"There are, unfortunately," she told Alice, "very few men like Vern."

Gloria had walked away from her marriage with only her personal possessions. She'd wanted nothing, not even memories, of the man she'd discovered having wild, abandoned sex with his secretary. But she'd wanted too much.

She remembered. She remembered how Charles had used her. In the end, she'd learned he'd never really wanted her as a woman. He'd only been interested in her excellent social skills to advance his social and corporate ambitions. He'd used her as his live-in hostess.

And she remembered, too clearly, he'd never had such wild, abandoned sex with her.

Alice came into Gloria's office carrying two steaming cups. Gloria accepted one with thanks.

"Vern's a rare one, right enough," Alice agreed. "But there's someone out there for you, dearie, never you fret. 'Course," she said, turning a bland look on her former charge, "they're not going to flock to your door. You've got to look for them, you know."

Gloria took a sip of her hot tea. "Yeah. Under a rock."

"Actually, I met my Vern on the bus," Alice said. "He helped me with my parcels."

Gloria sighed. Alice attracted gentlemen and *she* attracted oglers.

"Your nine o'clock appointment is Mr. and Mrs. Crenshaw," Alice said. "They've been invited to have dinner with the governor. Mr. Bodene is due at eleven." She frowned. "And you've scheduled Mr. Anderson through your lunchtime again," she said sternly.

Gloria shrugged. "He's an important client, and it was the only time he had."

"And of course he's uptight about this meeting coming up in Italy."

"Of course."

Alice frowned. "That leaves you with no lunch hour, you know, because after Mr. Anderson you have your table etiquette class, and after *that* is your social correspondence group."

"I brought a sandwich. I'll survive." Alice's concern warmed her. "Honest."

"I can stay in if you need me."

"And miss your lunch with Vern? Not on your life! One of us has to have some romance, and it looks like that falls to you."

Luke glared at the front page of the *Tidewater Daily News*. In bold print that seemed to him unnecessarily large, the words They're At It Again called the reader's attention to a black-and-white photo of a man and a woman in evening dress, facing each other almost nose to nose. Both their expressions were tight with fury.

Luke thrust himself up out of his executive chair and paced to the large window. It afforded a view of brilliant azure sky studded with fleecy clouds and, beyond breeze-stirred palms and ornate buildings, the blue waters of the Gulf of Mexico.

The newspaper story was familiar. Too damn familiar. Everyone in Tidewater must know about the animosity between his younger brother and the former Mrs. Joshua Cahill by now. How could they not? It seemed to Luke that these public arguments took place with distasteful regularity. Couldn't Josh and his ex-wife learn to keep their rancor private?

His intercom buzzed, and he stabbed the button.

"Your brother is here," his secretary said.

Luke frowned as he cast the paper a last glance. "Thank you, Claire. Send him in."

Josh walked into the office. Like Luke, he bore the stamp of the Cahill clan in height, fair coloring and classic bone structure. As he regarded his brother, younger by three years, Luke reflected that the Cahill men had never had trouble getting the women of their choice. His jaw tightened. The problem was they always chose the wrong women.

Claire quietly pulled the door closed, leaving the brothers alone.

"Mornin', Luke," Josh said, flashing a smile that had never failed to charm teachers from kindergarten through college. At twenty-nine, he could still use it to his advantage. Usually.

Josh caught sight of the newspaper lying on the large oak-and-leather desk. Instantly, his gaze cut to his brother standing by the window.

"Luke, I swear to you—I didn't know anyone from the press was there," Josh said, jumping immediately to his own defense.

Luke turned to face Josh, controlling his temper and concealing his bone-deep embarrassment by an exercise of will he'd had cause to learn since youth. Their father, Daniel Cahill, had also taken an inappropriate bride.

"Damn it, Josh, you were at a big annual fund-raiser. It doesn't take a rocket scientist to figure out the press would be there. They're there every year. They're *supposed* to be there. You represented all of us and you made a public spectacle of yourself. You made the Cahills look foolish. Again." Luke suddenly realized how tense his muscles had grown.

Bright fuchsia rose up Josh's neck to stain his face. "What gives you the right to dress me down like I was some wet-behind-the-ears kid caught peein' on the neighbor's petunias? I'm a grown man, and I don't need you to tell me how to behave!"

Luke merely lifted one eyebrow.

Josh's color deepened. After a moment, he looked away, venting a harsh sigh. "Aw, hell." He dragged his hand through his blond hair. "She provoked me."

"I never doubted that. But you allowed her to succeed."

Josh turned an angry look on Luke. "What do you know about it? You've never even been married."

And, Luke thought darkly, things would stay that way until he could find the *right* woman. Someone capable of exercising discretion. Someone who knew how to conduct herself with decorum. Someone who knew one damned fork from another. No more public humiliation. He wasn't going to repeat his father's and brother's mistakes.

"If you mean I've never conducted a whirlwind, one-night courtship, complete with a wedding conducted by an Elvis impersonator, you're right," he snapped.

"You just aren't going to let me forget that, are you? I told you, that was Bunnie's idea."

Another tasteful inspiration from the Vegas showgirl.

Josh looked down at the carpet and shook his head. When he looked up, he was smiling. "I can hardly wait until *you* fall in love. She'll probably be the bimbo of the century and will insist on the biggest, gaudiest, tackiest wedding in the history of Tidewater." His eyes gleamed. "And she'll invite every reporter from every media within a hundred-mile radius."

The very thought of what Josh described made Luke faintly ill. "No way, little brother."

"No?" Josh sat down in one of the deep leather chairs facing Luke's desk. He settled back comfortably with a theatrical sigh. "Well, maybe you're right. In fact, maybe you'll never marry at all. Maybe you're destined to be just a bachelor uncle." He folded his arms behind his head and regarded Luke. "Bunnie may not have been the wisest choice I've ever made, but at least she left me with Poppy. For that I will be eternally thankful."

Bright, cheerful, loving Poppy, Josh's six-year-old daughter, was the sunshine in the lives of the three Cahill men and of Daniel's widowed sister, Maudie. More than for her lack of taste or for her mortifying public displays, Luke disliked Bunnie for not making more of an effort to spend time with Poppy, her own daughter. For hurting that precious child, Luke could not forgive her.

"Now," Josh continued, "if you've finally got the commercial real-estate division moved in and straightened out, I've come to discuss a project." He grinned. "*Some* of us at Cahill Companies have work to do."

Gloria glanced at her watch as she took a bite of her bologna sandwich. Twelve o'clock and no Mr. Anderson. This was so unlike him. The man was obsessive about punctuality. Usually he arrived a few minutes early.

The office was quiet. Mr. Bodene had left promptly after their session, and Alice had gone to lunch. At least Gloria had a few minutes to eat her scanty meal in peace.

She heard the door to Hamilton Consulting open. Quickly she rewrapped her sandwich and walked out to greet Mr. Anderson.

"You!" The word exploded from her throat.

"Hello." The ogler smiled at her. "I've come to apologize."

Earlier, her red fury had inhibited her powers of observation, and she'd come away from her confrontation with little more than an impression of a handsome man. Now Gloria permitted herself a better look.

He was tall, very tall, and his precisely tailored gray suit revealed broad shoulders and long, lean limbs. His hair was a bit too long to be fashionable these days. Its color brought to Gloria's mind the ancient treasure of some fierce Norse raider: sparkling gold, threaded through with glints of silver and rare amber.

His classic features were flawlessly sculpted. Well, almost flawlessly. His otherwise perfect nose was just a bit crooked, as if it had once been broken. But his mouth was, without a doubt, quite flawless. Better than flawless. His mouth was superb. His mouth was...smiling.

Suddenly aware that she'd been staring at a stranger's mouth, Gloria felt a hot flush sweep her cheeks. She looked up into startling light blue eyes and found amusement. Her hackles rose.

"That's not at all necessary," she informed him coolly. "I've already seen what your apology is worth."

"I said I was apologizing. I never said I was blind."

"Or mannerly."

He arched a golden eyebrow. "Look, I admire a beautiful woman as much as the next man, but I usually don't...uh..." He appeared to be searching for a word.

"Ogle?" she supplied sweetly.

He had the grace to flush. "Yes, I guess that *is* what I've been doing, isn't it?" His color deepened. "I don't, normally. Ogle, that is. I mean, I may *look,* but I don't ogle."

"You *followed* me for three mornings, counting today."

He shrugged one shoulder. "It's just a matter of my happening to go to work the same time as you do. Nothing intentional about it. I wasn't plotting to arrive at the precise moment you did."

"You *followed* me," she repeated.

"I work in this building."

She folded her arms over her chest and stared him in the eye.

"All right! All...right," he said, huffing. "I admit I preferred to walk behind you."

She waited.

He idly looked down at his shoes. Silence filled the office. Then he peered up at her through thick blond lashes. Unrepentant devilment danced in his eyes. "The view was exceptional."

Something about his attitude, or his words—or maybe it was his cloudless-summer-sky eyes—slipped past her defenses. She found she was pleased that an attractive, desirable man found her attractive and desirable. Sternly she tried to squash that response. Her urge to laugh at his naughty-boy teasing, however, was harder to contend with. A smile almost escaped before she caught it.

He lifted his head and met her gaze squarely. "Please accept my apology." His perfect mouth curved up, slightly higher on one side than the other. "I promise I won't follow you again."

Against her better judgment, she found she wanted to believe him. A wicked little voice at the back of her mind whispered, *Let's see how charming he can be.* And Gloria was willing to bet he could be very charming indeed.

Clearly she shouldn't trust her judgment around this fellow. She'd bet her silver oyster forks that he wasn't nearly as sincere as he looked. And now that she thought of it, neighbors of serial killers were always saying things like: "Everybody liked him. Who would have thought he'd stuff all those women through his automatic wood chipper?"

"By the way," he said, holding his hand out to her, "I'm Luke Cahill."

Cahill. Why did that name sound vaguely familiar? She hesitated. What was she going to do? Call the police and report that an ogler had apologized and now wanted to shake her hand?

Unwilling to be rude, she clasped his hand. "Gloria Hamilton."

His long fingers closed around hers. They were warm and strong. As if he sensed her uncertainty, he kept the shake gracefully brief, releasing her smoothly.

"Glad to meet you, Gloria Hamilton. Are you the proprietor of Hamilton Consulting?"

"Yes." Surely she could think of something more scintillating than just one single-syllable word. "Yes, I am." *Oh, brilliant.*

"Have you eaten lunch yet?" he asked.

Her hollow stomach convinced Gloria that one bite of bologna sandwich didn't qualify as lunch. "No. Actually, I was just—"

"Then would you do me the honor of joining me for lunch? My treat. A peace offering."

He fixed her with that blue gaze again, and Gloria thought how easy it would be to just dive in and drift away.

"Let's start fresh," he coaxed, his low, masculine voice gliding over her like a silken net of persuasion.

Oh, the temptation.

"I . . . can't."

He regarded her evenly. "You don't trust me, do you?" he asked quietly.

It wasn't as if she believed he had a wood chipper stashed somewhere. No, she just felt . . . well, he wasn't her type. That was it, of course. He wasn't her type. Luke Cahill was much too unpredictable.

"Trust has nothing to do with the matter," she informed him primly.

A knowing smile slid across his wonderful mouth. "Then prove it."

"Prove it?" she echoed.

He nodded, his eyes never leaving hers. "Come to lunch with me now. I know where we can find a table overlooking the water."

Gloria felt his magnetism tug at her. A part of her wanted to toss wisdom and responsibility to the wind and dash, laughing, out the door with this man. Fortunately, that part wasn't in control of her motor functions.

"I'm afraid I already have plans for my lunchtime."

Behind Luke, the door opened.

"I'm sorry I'm late, Gloria," Wade Anderson said, slightly short of breath, as if he'd run all the way from the parking garage. "Traffic tie-up. I hope you still have some time for me."

Gloria saw the way in which Luke regarded Mr. Anderson. She didn't miss the slight narrowing of his eyes. Nor did she miss the sharp light of speculation as he studied the other man. Not for the first time, Gloria noticed that her client was attractive. Today she was especially glad for his dark good looks. Just let Mr. Cahill speculate all he liked. If he believed Wade was her luncheon date, so much the better.

"We have plenty of time, Wade. Go on back, if you will, and I'll join you in a second."

But apparently his lack of punctuality was preying on Mr. Anderson. "Gloria, I do apologize for arriving so late for our review." He acknowledged Luke's presence with a quick, stiff smile, then headed down the short hall to the room she used for one-on-one "reviews."

In truth, there was no review. She knew the lessons involved information new to her clients. She also kept in mind how embarrassing it might be to admit complete or even partial ignorance of protocol, customs or etiquette, particularly for businesspeople. So she referred to her lessons as consultations or reviews. Some of her clients liked to call the sessions "briefings." That was okay, too.

When Mr. Anderson left, she turned back to Luke. To her embarrassment, his lips curled in a knowing smile.

"Seems to be your day to receive apologies," he said softly.

"Thank you for coming by," she stated stiffly. "I've got to go now."

"Yes, I can see that. But before you start your, er, review—what *is* it that you do here?"

"I'm an etiquette-and-protocol consultant," she explained. "I really must go now."

She turned and hurried down the hall. When she didn't hear the door open, she looked back over her shoulder.

Luke was watching her walk away with great interest.

Righteous indignation boiled up in her. So much for his apologies! She fixed him with an angry scowl and pointed to the door behind him. *"Out!"*

He held up his hands as if to ward off her wrath. "I'm going, I'm going."

"You, sir, are—"

"I know." He sighed. "A swine."

Chapter Two

"It's a pig." Gloria stared at the small, beautifully crafted charm lying in the open velvet-lined box on Alice's desk.

Alice nodded in agreement. "Quite." She smoothed out the rumpled brown paper in which the jeweler's box had arrived at the office. "No return address."

Gloria picked up the charm between thumb and forefinger, holding the minuscule porker up to the light of the window in the waiting area. Faceted gold winked in the sunshine.

"This is most puzzling," Alice mused. "Who would send you such an odd, but costly gift—" she wrinkled her nose as she eyed the pig "—and not include their return address?"

Minute sapphire eyes seemed to return Gloria's gaze. Pig...

I know. A swine.

Her eyebrows drew down.

He wouldn't.

Then she remembered those compelling blue eyes. That once-broken nose. His devilish, crooked smile.

He would.

Her mouth tightened. "I believe I know who sent this."

Alice's face brightened with interest. "Oh?"

Gloria nodded slowly, studying the expensive trinket. "Uh-huh."

"And . . . ?" the secretary hinted broadly.

But Gloria didn't want to discuss her encounter with Luke Cahill just yet. For some reason, it seemed . . . well . . . private, as if they'd been alone on the planet instead of merely alone in the office for those few minutes. On the other hand, the experience had been exasperating. He had been exasperating. No, irritating, she told herself. *Irritating* was a better word for that tall, blond Texan.

She placed the gold figure back in its elegant box, then snapped the lid shut. "I could be wrong," she said as she headed back to her office. *But I doubt it.*

As Gloria researched protocol for a client's upcoming business trip to Brazil, she found her gaze returning to the box on the corner of her desk. She couldn't keep the gift, of course. It wasn't proper to accept jewelry from strange men. And wasn't that what she'd always been? Proper?

Only—she reached out and opened the moiré-silk-covered lid—he didn't really seem like a stranger. A peculiar intimacy existed between them. Honesty forced her to admit that he was outside of any previous experience she'd ever had with men. She caressed the tiny pig with the tip of a forefinger. He knew she'd been angry. Was this yet another apology? After all, he hadn't been on the elevator this morning. A show of good faith? Or a morning appointment?

Gloria withdrew her finger and straightened slightly in her chair. Whatever his plan was, it wouldn't work.

Exactly what did she know about Luke Cahill, anyway? She knew his name. He'd told her he worked in this building. The cut and quality of his suit had connoted success. And without a doubt, Luke was good to look at. She glanced over at the gold charm. Also, the man was unconventional.

Gloria didn't like that. She'd always felt a need to plan. That was the way to be in control of things. Of life.

Quickly she flicked the box closed. She would return the charm to him, and that would be the end to this whole ridiculous episode.

A dentist's appointment made Luke an hour and a half late getting to the office.

"Morning, Claire," he said, passing his secretary at her desk on the way to his office. "By the way, thank you for tracking down the office of that tenant I asked you about yesterday."

"You're quite welcome, Mr. Cahill," she replied, refusing as ever to call him by his first name, regardless of his request. "Mr. Ramsey's messenger came by. The envelope is on your desk."

"Excellent," he said with great satisfaction. He absently accepted the stack of pink telephone messages she handed him, thinking that Henry Ramsey could always be counted on. "Please hold my calls."

Luke quietly closed the double mahogany doors of his office behind him and crossed the carpet to his desk. There, as Ramsey had promised him late yesterday afternoon, lay the report on Gloria Hamilton.

He still remembered the frisson of excitement that had shot through his body when she had stepped into the waiting area of her office. She was not quite what he'd imagined, and yet... she was.

He found himself genuinely attracted to her, and under all that angry indignation, he believed she felt at least a nascent attraction to him. When he looked into those sherry brown eyes, he'd forgotten about her perfect, lush little fanny, about her long, gorgeous legs up to *there*. Maybe not completely forgotten, but something had arced between them. Something... personal. An inexplicable, intangible *something* that had shimmered through his usual defenses.

Luke didn't believe in love at first sight. That hogwash was the invention of troubadours looking for an easy meal. He wasn't sure he believed in romantic love at all; it hadn't worked for his parents or his brother, and divorce was rife everywhere. But he firmly believed in the love of family. He believed in the bond of faith between true friends. And, after yesterday, he might even believe—just a little—in magic.

He circled his massive desk and sat down in the brown leather executive chair, staring bemusedly at the envelope. He'd never asked for a report from Henry Ramsey on a woman before. At least, not a social acquaintance. Though he had requested a few reports before, they had always been issued on persons involved with Luke's business. Prospects. Clients. Competitors.

Now Luke had before him such an account on Gloria Hamilton. It made him feel lower than a snake's belly to have commissioned the thing, but there was a purpose, he told himself sternly. He needed to know more about her.

He pulled the report from the envelope.

"So, you like that new project idea," Josh said, settling back in his chair at their sidewalk café table. The restaurant was a favorite lunch spot on Jetty Avenue across the street from the Grimble Building. He eyed his empty plate, then cast his gaze to Luke's french fries. "Are you going to eat those?"

"Yes, I'm going to eat them. If you want more, order some." Luke finished the last bite of his club sandwich and sighed with contentment. The autumn sunshine felt good. A soft breeze off the Gulf ruffled his hair. "God, it's a beautiful day."

Josh cocked a sandy eyebrow. "It must be love."

Luke flushed slightly. "I don't know about that—"

Josh sat bolt upright. "Aha! I knew it!" he crowed triumphantly. "You couldn't hold out forever." He rubbed his hands together in avid anticipation. "Okay, so who is she? Oh, boy, this is gonna be good!"

"Try to show a little enthusiasm, will you?" Luke said dryly.

"After all these years of razzing from you, I'm finally going to get my turn. And don't think I won't take full advantage of the situation."

Unexpectedly, out of the corner of his eye, Luke caught sight of a slim, nicely curved figure striding down the sidewalk, coming toward him. He turned his head, compelled to focus on her by some peculiar inner need, easily picking Gloria out of the lunchtime foot traffic.

Elegant as usual, she was dressed today in a suit of yellow silk, and her dark hair was in its customary smooth twist at the top of her nape.

He knew the instant she discovered him. Her chin lifted fractionally. Then she haughtily gazed straight ahead, continuing on a course that would take her right by the sidewalk café where he sat with Josh.

Luke grinned. Damn, she had spirit.

"So who's the lucky lady?" Josh asked again, plucking a french fry from Luke's plate. "What bimbo has captured the heretofore unerring Cahill's heart?"

"There, on the sidewalk, coming this way. The gorgeous female in yellow. Dark hair."

Josh looked. And frowned. "She doesn't dress like a bimbo," he accused. "Do I have the right one? She's wearing a suit? And black high heels?"

Luke smiled smugly. "That's her."

"Well, this can't be love. It just can't be. I'd swear *she's* a lady. Look, she doesn't even wiggle very much when she walks." Josh turned back to Luke. Defiantly he snatched another fry. "She's probably sexually repressed," he suggested darkly.

Luke threw back his head and laughed. "You think so?" Not with the fiery temper she had. No, there was definitely passion in Gloria Hamilton.

Josh swallowed his fry. "Well, as I said, this can't be love."

Luke's eyes sought her out again, and he watched her move among the other pedestrians as she drew nearer to the café. "It's not." Not love, maybe, but something. A chemistry, certainly. But something else. Something more elusive. He thought his inability to put his finger on this whatever-it-was should bother him, yet he found himself content to accept what was happening. For the moment.

"What do you mean, it's not love?" Josh demanded. "So there's nothing going on?"

"Oh, yes. There's plenty going on. I'm just not going to lose my head over anyone." He reluctantly took his gaze from Gloria to face Josh. "I'm going to make absolutely certain of this woman before I marry her."

On the other side of the hip-high, wrought-iron fencing that separated the café premises from the sidewalk, Gloria drew abreast of their table without acknowledging Luke.

"Good afternoon, Gloria," he said pleasantly.

She looked at him then, her eyes flashing. "Good afternoon, Mr. Cahill," she replied shortly, not pausing in her stride. In a second, she'd passed them by.

Amusement danced in Josh's eyes. "Oh, yeah. You make real sure of this woman before you marry her, big brother. Maybe you'll discover that she obviously hates your guts before you make it to the altar."

Luke leaned back in his chair. "Well, I'm working on it," he allowed sheepishly.

"How?"

"First I want to make certain of her. Why waste a perfectly good courtship if she's not what I want?" He really wasn't ready to make a decision yet. At least, not an informed decision.

Josh arched an eyebrow.

"Or, if I'm not what she wants," Luke conceded.

"So what steps have you taken to make sure she's not some bimbo in disguise?"

"I had Ramsey do a rundown on her."

"You ordered a report on her?" Josh rolled his eyes. "You romantic, you."

"I told him not to run the financials," Luke objected, feeling guilty. He hadn't really wanted the report, but he was playing for keeps here and knew he had to exercise caution.

Josh shook his head. "I don't get it, Luke. You're the man who's made TGP so successful by keeping your competitors off-balance, by playing your hunches. Now you're selecting a bride with all the calculation of a tax auditor. It makes me wonder if you're the same person who climbed the trellis to quote sonnets to Cindy Morris and ask her to your junior prom."

Luke flushed. "She told you about that, did she?"

Josh grinned wickedly. "She told everyone about that."
He sobered. "Honestly, Luke, you can't go about picking
out a wife like she's a late-model Buick."

"Why not? It makes sense, doesn't it? Isn't that how
people used to get married? You wed a woman because her
property bordered yours, or because she had a fortune, or
because, by allying your family with hers, you could beat the
king or earl or whatever."

Josh scowled, seeming to have forgotten all about the
limp french fry he held. "That was in the Dark Ages! They
also used to drag unwilling women bound and gagged to the
altar."

"Might have eliminated an Elvis impersonator or two."

"Damn it, Luke—!"

"Never fear, Josh. If I decide she's the one, she'll come
to the altar willingly enough." Luke gazed in the direction
Gloria had been going, idly seeking a yellow suit in the
stream of colors that moved along the sidewalk. If she
proved to be the woman he wanted, he'd do what was necessary to make her want him.

Josh vented a frustrated sigh and tossed the fry down on
his plate. "My brother has gone nuts," he announced.
"Nuts."

"Look, so far everything I've found out indicates she'll
be perfect for me. She's intelligent, articulate and comes
from a good family—her father was a diplomat. She appears to lead a conservative sort of life. She's the owner of
Hamilton Consulting so she's bound to know which fork to
use." Luke met his brother's gaze squarely. "I'm ready to
marry, Josh, and I'm not taking any chances on winding up
with the usual Cahill bride."

As if summoned by his words, Bunnie Cahill stalked toward them. Luke took in her bright green, too-low-cut, too-
short, too-tight spandex dress, the patterned black stockings and the impossibly high, pink stiletto-heeled sandals.
He glanced at her wild, bleached-white mane and wondered how a woman could go to one of Tidewater's most

expensive beauty salons and still come out looking like a five-dollar hooker.

From her taut expression, it was clear that Bunnie was angry about something, and that something probably had a connection to her ex-husband. She halted at their table, her feet planted wide as if for battle.

"I thought I'd find you here," she snarled at Josh. "Where's my alimony check?"

"Charming as ever," Luke observed mildly.

Her head snapped around. Her emerald eyes narrowed at him. "Well, if it isn't Mr. Holier-Than-Thou. I'm amazed you're willing to mingle with the common people."

Luke smiled icily. "Some more common than others, it appears."

"Bastard!" she hissed. "You always thought I wasn't good enough for your precious Cahill name, didn't you?"

"Actually, no."

She looked confused. Confusion altered into suspicion. "What is *that* supposed to mean?" She turned to Josh. "What does he mean?"

"It means, dearest, that he never thought our esteemed name too good for you. You're what he expected. In fact, he believes you have a few things in common with our mother."

Bunnie bristled instantly. "Your mother's a tramp! I'm not like her at all." Her eyes glistened with moisture. "Josh, I never cheated on you. Never."

He gently took her right hand in his. "I know, sweetheart. I know."

Luke pushed back his chair and stood. "I'll leave you two to your discussion. Bunnie—" he gave her a curt nod "—a pleasure, as always."

She sniffled. "Go to hell, Luke."

Instead of abiding by Bunnie's wish, Luke went instead to a pay telephone down the sidewalk. He withdrew a piece of paper from the inside pocket of his cobalt blue linen jacket and dialed the number.

"Hamilton Consulting," said a woman's English-accented voice.

Luke inquired into the firm's schedule and enrolled in the only class set for that evening—a class on table manners. As he hung up the phone, someone in the crowd jostled him. Alert to the ways of pickpockets, Luke quickly checked to make sure he had his wallet. Again he was jostled, and he sharply scanned the faces around him to no avail. He headed toward the Grimble Building. His temper calmed as he remembered he'd be seeing Gloria that evening. As he strolled into the lobby, he whistled the old Jimmy Buffett tune, "Cheeseburger in Paradise."

At seven o'clock, Gloria walked into the larger of the consultation rooms, which was painted a light, cheerful yellow and decorated with potted weeping fig trees and antique-framed watercolors by local artists. Tonight the yellow room was furnished with two long tables set end to end and draped with white tablecloths. Ten places had each been arrayed with a cloth dinner napkin, dishes, flatware and glasses of various kinds. At every setting sat an adult student.

She looked around the room, smiling at each of her students—until she came to the tall blond man seated last at the second table.

Her smile froze. Luke Cahill grinned back at her.

She checked her enrollment list, hoping there had been a mistake. There hadn't. His name appeared at the bottom of the list.

There was no help for it now. She couldn't very well eject him from the office, though that particular little fantasy held a certain appeal. She'd just have to play along and hope that he didn't become disruptive.

She went through her usual opening about this class being a fun experience, but also good practice for that next state dinner at the White House or formal repast with the governor. That brought some laughter from people who clearly were not anticipating such invitations, which helped to relax everyone.

At each place setting was a small, hand-painted name card. Couples had been separated, as they would be at a formal dinner. She explained the practical purpose behind such seating arrangements. "Husbands and wives aren't seated together because they might be inclined to discuss the same old things they always talk about—kids, bills and neighbors. How much fun would that be for anyone?" More chuckles.

She proceeded to the table settings themselves, explaining as she moved about the room, smiling easily.

"At a formal dinner, the napkin is always arranged on the place plate." With a sweep of her open hand, she indicated the large white damask napkins she and Alice had folded into simple rectangles.

She stopped at the place of the woman sitting next to Luke. Hannah Gilder, according to the place card. Gloria guessed her to be in her mid-sixties. She was obviously nervous. Gloria lightly rested her hand on Mrs. Gilder's shoulder and gave it a slight, encouraging squeeze. Mrs. Gilder managed a smile.

As Gloria walked around the end of the table, she could feel Luke's gaze follow her. It made her stomach flutter.

Now stop that! she scolded herself. *Just pretend he's not even here.*

Fat chance.

She picked up the dinner napkin from her own place setting, determined not to let Luke Cahill's presence rattle her. Out of the corner of her eye, she sneaked a peek at him. Slowly he smiled.

With a will, she redirected her attention to her other students. "Take the lower left corner of the napkin, picking up the first two layers. Like so." The cloth she held up opened easily, yet remained folded once, lengthwise. "Now, just drape it over your lap." She watched with satisfaction as all of her students flawlessly executed the opening and placing of their napkins.

Everyone, that is, except Mrs. Gilder. She dropped hers. Luke caught it before it hit the floor and quietly, unobtrusively, returned the napkin to the flustered woman.

"You never completely open the napkin," Gloria continued smoothly. "And you never snap it open."

After she explained the arrangement and purpose of the multiple forks, knives, spoons and glasses, she walked to the wall and pressed the intercom button.

"Okay, Fred," she said softly to the caterer set up in the next room. "We're ready for the first course."

The consommé went without a hitch, aside from a few slurping noises, quickly corrected by the guilty party—a young man in a business suit.

Next came the fish. Each student was served a platter upon which resided a fried rainbow trout, complete with head and tail. One woman made a small, distressed sound and another made a face.

"Imagine how *they* must feel about it," Gloria teased, then went on to demonstrate how to sever the head and separate the meat from the bones with knife and fork.

She strolled from student to student, assisting and instructing and encouraging conversation between them. When she arrived at the end of the second table, she was relieved to see Mrs. Gilder had so far managed to remove the head and was working on the remaining portion of the fish. Gloria praised the accomplishment, and the older woman acknowledged it with a pleased blush.

Luke looked up at Gloria with too-innocent eyes. "Oh, Ms. Hamilton, I need help."

Gloria glanced at his expertly carved fish. "Yes, Mr. Cahill," she said sweetly, "you certainly do." She leaned down so that their conversation could not be overheard. "What is it with you?" she whispered furiously. "You promised not to follow me, remember?"

"Follow you?" he asked. "I'm not following you. I need help with my table manners."

"Oh, sure. And Arthur Murray needs dance lessons. The manners you need help with have nothing to do with consommé or trout."

He turned slightly so he could look at her. "I've been a model student," he objected. "All I've done is sit here absorbing each little gem of knowledge that's tumbled off your lips." As if under a control other than his own, his eyes lowered to her lips. Quickly he jerked them back up.

His breath was warm against her cheek and smelled of butter and herbs. Inexplicably, Gloria was intensely aware of broad, masculine shoulders clothed in dark linen, of a firm mouth with a perfect bowed upper lip, and of thick gold hair shot with silver blond and amber.

"You don't happen to have a wood chipper, do you?" she asked, not quite meeting his eyes.

His expression betrayed his confusion. "Wood chipper? Why would I have a wood chipper?"

"Never mind," she muttered, straightening, feeling the need to put some distance between them. She absently waved her hand in the direction of the remainder of the fish on his plate. "Keep up the good work."

"I intend to."

Startled, she did meet his eyes. In their crystal blue depths she found amusement, invitation.

Fred and his assistant entered the room to remove the remains of the fish course. Almost immediately they returned bearing platters of Cornish game hens, which had been done to a crisp brown turn.

"Ordinarily," she told her students, "this course would be beef, or some other equally easy-to-deal-with meat. So I chose these little game hens, which are more of a challenge and have caused many uncomfortable moments for the uninitiated."

She demonstrated how to anchor and cut, then invited the class members to follow her example. The game hens proved more difficult, as she had expected they would. It was, however, important that her students learn to carve them, because such small birds were not uncommon on formal dinner menus.

She caught a glimpse of Mrs. Gilder's struggle, and started toward her to offer help. Again, the older woman tried to anchor with her fork, stabbing determinedly at the hen. The small bird carcass shot off her platter and rocketed across the room.

Instantly, Luke switched plates with the red-faced lady.

The missile crashed against the wall and dropped to the carpet. Everyone turned to see who had been so clumsy.

There sat Luke with an empty plate. He smiled apologetically. "Oops."

There was a smattering of embarrassed laughter before everyone quickly riveted their gazes back to their own plates.

Mrs. Gilder stared down at the game hen, blinking rapidly. Then she looked over at Luke. She opened her mouth twice to speak and failed both times. Gloria saw him wink at Mrs. Gilder, who laughed despite herself, though that short sound held a choked quality.

Gloria didn't want to call attention to Mrs. Gilder's acute distress by going over to her right now. Yet, if that lady didn't learn how to carve a small bird, Gloria would feel she'd failed her student.

She surveyed the room. No one was looking toward the end of table number two. As she casually started in Mrs. Gilder's direction, she found that Luke had moved his chair a little closer to his neighbor and was quietly, patiently, showing her how to contend with a crisp Cornish game hen.

The vegetable course and dessert course followed without mishap, and finally the members of her class sauntered out the door. As they passed the reception desk in the waiting area, many of them took one or more of the caterer's business cards.

While Fred and his assistant cleared away the dinner mess, Gloria attended to the wall and carpet that had been assaulted by Mrs. Gilder's hen. Not fifteen minutes later, the two men wheeled their loaded stainless-steel carts out of Hamilton Consulting. She walked out with them, purse under her arm, and locked the door behind her. They arrived at the elevator to find Luke Cahill waiting.

"I thought I'd walk you to your car, Ms. Hamilton," he said. "I didn't want you to have to make the trip to the parking garage by yourself."

"Thank you, but on the evenings of my Ease At The Table class, Fred and one of his associates always escort me." He really could be a very considerate, even sensitive, man, she thought, remembering how he'd twice come to the aid of the embarrassed Mrs. Gilder. "You're welcome to join us, isn't that right, Fred? Nick?" Both men politely agreed, and Gloria performed the introductions.

The elevator doors opened, and the caterers trundled the carts on board, accompanied by the clatter and clink of dishes. Gloria and Luke followed.

Silence surrounded them all the way down to the ground floor and out to the curb, where Nick had earlier parked the catering company's panel truck. The carts were quickly loaded inside. After the four passengers climbed in, Fred drove the panel truck to the parking garage, stopped at Gloria's car and wished her good-night.

Luke got out, too, helping her down. He thanked the other men for the lift.

"Luke," Fred said in a no-nonsense tone of voice, "I can drop you off at your car." His meaning was clear. He didn't like leaving this near-stranger alone with Gloria.

"It's okay, Fred," Gloria said softly. "You're a doll."

With obvious reluctance, Fred drove away, the engine echoing loudly against the concrete walls of the parking garage. Moments later, silence fell again.

"I don't think Fred trusts me," Luke complained, feigning hurt. "Is he your brother?"

Gloria laughed. "No."

"You could have fooled me."

She looked down at the keys in her hand, then up at Luke. "I did a little coaching with Fred when he had his heart set on a woman whose family thought he'd be an embarrassment to them, since there was such a disparity in their social standing. They placed him in a few situations—formal dinners, country weekends with real movers and shakers in the state, stuff like that—and expected him to fall flat on his face. But he didn't. In fact, he was quite a hit. Anyway, in the end he got the girl. He persists in giving me all the credit, which of course is an utter fallacy."

Luke leaned on his elbow against the roof of her old sedan. Irrationally, Gloria was glad for the low lighting in the garage. Maybe he wouldn't notice that her car wasn't in keeping with the image she tried to project for Hamilton Consulting. The car was definitely past its prime, but as long as it still ran, she wouldn't have to make car payments. Her business needed all her capital.

He shifted his weight from one foot to the other, which brought him slightly closer to her. "And now Fred is catering your table-manners class."

She shrugged. "He's a good caterer. His food is wonderful, and I know I can count on him." Luke's proximity was having an effect on her central nervous system. Her heart rate was picking up. "I prefer dealing with people I can count on."

He smiled. "Doesn't everyone?"

For a moment, she thought she glimpsed a shadow of sadness in those light eyes. "Yes," she answered, "I suppose that's true."

She suddenly remembered something and dug around in her purse until she found what she was seeking. "I must return this to you." She held out the small jeweler's box to him.

He made no move to accept it. "Didn't you like the charm?"

"Thank you for the thought, but I can't accept your gift." She continued to hold the box out to him.

His neutral expression revealed nothing of what he might be thinking. "Why?"

This man gave all the evidence of one well versed in social etiquette. She refused to believe him ignorant of the proprieties. "You know very well why not!"

"Humor me."

She was tempted to bounce the box off his head. "All right. This gift is much too personal," she informed him tartly. "I don't know you well enough to accept an item of jewelry."

"Queen Victoria would have been proud of you," he said dryly. "But it's not as if I gave you a black silk nightie or a jewel for your navel. It's a little charm."

"A little pig charm." And she thought it was adorable.

"Do you like my gift?"

She flushed and was thankful again for the low lights in the garage. "Yes, but that's not the point," she insisted.

"Tell me, Gloria—" he leaned fractionally closer "—what *is* the point?"

"This is simply too personal a gift," she repeated stubbornly, considering taking a step back, then rejecting the idea. Though he really wasn't invading her personal space, his presence was unnervingly strong. Commanding. She suspected that, without moving a muscle or uttering a word, this man could take control of any place or any situation. She preferred to be in control of her own places and situations. "I don't know you well enough to accept an article designed to be worn on my person." Good grief, that sounded stiff and prissy even to her ears.

His smile returned. Gloria noticed how Luke's slightly crooked nose saved his face from austere perfection by giving it a roguish quality.

"We can remedy that problem easily enough. Let's get better acquainted," he coaxed in a knee-melting baritone.

She shook her head. "I don't think that's a good idea."

"Oh? Why is that?"

How could she say what needed to be said without being rude, without hurting his feelings and without making herself look like a coward? She considered for a moment, then came to the conclusion that plain speaking was required. She drew a fortifying breath.

"We're two very different people. I doubt we have anything in common, other than we work in the same building and arrive at the same time."

Still smiling, he raised an eyebrow. "What makes you think we're so different?"

"You mean aside from the fact that the men I know wouldn't ogle a lady?"

"You know that for a fact, do you?"

Actually, she didn't. "All right, there's the matter of our basic personalities. I'm a quiet sort of person—"

"Oh? The quiet sort of person who tongue-lashes gentlemen on an elevator?"

She blushed furiously. "A man who spends three days staring at a woman's derriere is no gentleman."

His smile turned a bit wicked. "Ah, but such an attractive derriere would tempt any man to wayward behavior. And I have apologized."

"Twice. And neither time, I think, was exactly heartfelt."

"I regret having upset you, Gloria. And, as you will notice, I've reformed."

"There's also the matter of our life-styles," she said, forging on.

He laughed. "Life-styles? What could you possibly know about my life-style?" He wiggled his eyebrows at her. "Unless you've been doing research on me?"

"No," she said stiffly. "All I had to do was look at the front page of the newspaper yesterday."

His smile vanished. "That was my brother, not me."

"Yes, I know. And you weren't in the article about your mother last week, either, when she—never mind." Gloria looked down, fidgeting with the charm box in her hands. "I'm not saying anything but that you travel in more colorful circles than I do. You're bound to have a more...interesting life than mine. It's just that—"

"You're a snob," he said flatly.

Gloria jerked her head up. "No, I'm not! I—"

"Don't know a damn thing about the way I live." His shuttered face revealed nothing of his thoughts or emotions, but she heard anger seething in his words. "Tell me something. Have you ever seen *me* in the papers or on the television news?"

She blinked. "No."

"Did you even know who I was on the elevator yesterday?"

"No."

"Then what makes you such an authority on my life-style?" He sneered the last word.

Dear Lord, she'd hurt him. A knot of regret clutched Gloria's stomach. "The man in the sandwich shop..." Her words died on her lips. How could she have been so careless? So quick to judge?

"Oh, great. That's where *I* always go for information. The guy in the sandwich shop."

"You're right," she snapped defensively. He was the one who'd started all of this, she told herself. "Next time I want to know something about a—" She caught herself. *A man who intrigues me.* She certainly wasn't going to admit that! "A strange person, I guess I'll just go hire a detective. I hear that's done all the time now."

A muscle jumped in his jaw. "Yeah? Well, you seem to hear a lot of things that aren't necessarily based in fact."

She drew herself up and set one hand on the driver's door handle. She felt as if something might be slipping through her fingers, and she didn't want to think about it. "I'm sorry if I misjudged you," she said crisply. "Though you must admit, you gave me cause."

"Nice apology. So heartfelt."

"It's as good as any of yours."

His mouth curved up slightly. "Is this where I say 'Nanny, nanny, boo-boo'?"

She couldn't resist the smile that tugged at her mouth. "I guess it would be rather appropriate, wouldn't it?"

His smile deepened. "I'd rather invite you to a barbecue."

I'm not a snob, she told herself. But she'd learned to be cautious. She still doubted she and Luke had anything in common. Maybe spending a little time together would convince him, too, and no one's pride would be injured. That was the solution—she'd simply let nature take its course.

She returned Luke's smile. "I accept your invitation."

Chapter Three

"I need a favor from you, Aunt Maudie," Luke said as he carried the last of the dirty dinner dishes from the table into the kitchen the following evening.

Maudie Forsyth, his father's widowed sister, lived on the sprawling Cahill ranch just outside of Tidewater, along with her divorced brother, her two nephews and her one, adored great-niece. She was tall and slim and possessed the classic Cahill beauty that her fifty-five years had done little to dim. Her blond hair had turned to a soft silver.

Now as she stood at the sink on the maid's night off, she turned her blue eyes toward Luke and lifted a slender eyebrow. "I wondered why you were helping clear the table."

"I'm crushed. How could you imply that my good deed is prompted by an ulterior motive?"

Maudie laughed. "Easily. You hate anything to do with cleaning up after meals."

"I've helped before," he objected.

"Yes, you have. It's just the way you hold your mouth when you do it. As if your sensibilities are offended."

"But I *am* doing it," he insisted. "Wouldn't you know the blasted dishwasher would be broken."

Maudie smiled as she took the dishes from him and rinsed them off before submerging them in the bubble-covered water in one side of the double sink. "So what is this favor you want so badly that you'll help with the dishes?"

He pulled out a drawer and plucked a clean tea towel from a neatly folded stack. "I'd like the family to have a barbecue."

Maudie looked thoughtful as she briefly ran the disposal, then filled the other sink with clear hot water. "May I ask why you have this sudden interest in a family gathering?" She washed and rinsed a bowl, then handed it to him.

"It's been a while since we've had one." Luke all but polished the design off the bowl.

"I see." She washed several dishes and set them in the rinse water without saying another word.

Luke dried silverware, glasses and plates in determined silence. He knew what his aunt wanted to hear, and he was reluctant to part with the information. Maudie had been trying for years to marry him off to "a nice Southern girl." He didn't want to raise her hopes that he was about to tie the knot, but most of all, he didn't want any interference in what he was about to do. He knew his romantic aunt would disapprove. Still, if he wanted one of her all-out, down-home barbecues, he had to give her something. And he'd already invited Gloria.

He cleared his throat.

Not looking up from her work at the sink, Maudie said, "Yes?"

"There's a lady that I'd like to introduce to the family."

Instantly, Maudie straightened, her eyes bright. "Oh, Luke, that's wonderful!"

"Now, Aunt Maudie, it's probably not what you think. We haven't even dated yet. I want to see how she gets along with the family first."

Maudie sighed. "Sometimes I despair for you, Luke. How can such a handsome young man be so *un*romantic?"

Luke met his aunt's gaze. He'd been romantic once, and look what it had gotten him. "I don't see that romance ever did a lot for Dad or Josh. Or Uncle Riley, or Uncle Merl, or Grandpa, or—"

"I get the picture."

He looked down at the dinner plate he was rubbing with the damp terry towel. "I want my children to have a real mother, one who will love them and care for them. I want a wife I can be proud of." He lifted his gaze and found understanding in his aunt's eyes. "I'm going to select my wife very carefully. I want a lady, Maudie. A real lady."

They worked in silence for a few minutes. The only sound in the big kitchen was the clinking of dishes as Luke stacked them on the long oak worktable, uncertain where everything went.

"When do you want to have the barbecue?" Maudie asked.

"Weekend after next."

Maudie frowned thoughtfully. "That doesn't give me much time, but I think I can manage, if you help."

"Anything," Luke offered promptly. "Just tell me what you need me to do."

"You've already invited her, haven't you?"

Luke felt his face warm. "Uh, yeah."

"She must really be something. What's her name?"

"Promise you won't say anything about this to anyone?"

Maudie slipped her hand out of the yellow rubber glove and drew a large X over her heart with her forefinger. "Cross my heart."

"Her name is Gloria Hamilton." Gloria Hamilton with the compelling gaze and intriguing voice. And the shapeliest little fanny in Texas.

Somehow, Luke managed to withstand his aunt's gentle interrogation without rendering any other details. Considering Maudie's skill at extracting information from her menfolk, he believed that to be no small accomplishment.

After they finished the dishes, he went into the media room, where he found his niece watching her favorite cartoon tape on the large-screen television.

"What's this?" he said in a mock-gruff voice. "Have you done all your homework, young lady?"

Six-year-old Poppy giggled and shook her head. Two long blond braids swirled at her waist. "No, Uncle Luke. I don't have any homework."

He sat down on the ottoman next to the child. "Well, I'm just going to have to have a talk with that teacher of yours. First-graders should have to do homework. She's not working you hard enough."

Large, shamrock green eyes twinkled with delight. She leaned her small shoulder against his side, and Luke felt his heart expand.

"Will you play Candyland with me?" she asked.

Luke thought of the pile of papers on his desk in the study that demanded his attention. "All right. But only one game."

She gave him a gap-toothed smile. "Two," she coaxed. "Two games, *ple-e-ease?*"

He tapped the tip of her lightly freckled nose. "Okay, two. But then I have to do *my* homework."

Poppy ran to retrieve the box that held the game board and pieces. They set the board out on the antique, hand-hooked carpet in the family room. As their tokens progressed around the board, their shared laughter firmed Luke's resolve. God, he wanted this child to be happy all the time. If only she'd been born to a woman who gave a damn. His jaw tightened. There was little he could do to replace the mother who neglected Poppy, but he could make certain that the woman *he* married wanted children. That she would treasure them for the gifts they were. And perhaps, if he was very careful in his selection, his chosen mate would spread her love and nurturing to Poppy. This adorable child would learn the ways of a lady as she grew into graceful womanhood beside his own daughters.

His daughters. Luke smiled as a warmth spread through his chest at the thought.

But first he had to find the right wife.

Surely it wasn't asking too much to want a woman he could be proud of? A woman who practiced the social graces with ease, who could mingle with the families of old money or new, yet who wasn't a snob.

Gloria Hamilton might be a snob, but he doubted it. Even in the dim light of the parking garage, he'd seen her regret when she'd thought she'd hurt his feelings. Oh, she might be a bit prudish, but he could help her get over that. It would be a distinct pleasure helping her to get over that.

"I win, Uncle Luke!" Poppy cried triumphantly.

"Oh, yeah?"

Poppy beamed. "Yeah."

Luke lowered his head to rub noses with his niece. "Okay, but you won't tell anyone, will you?"

"I'm going to tell Daddy right now!" she crowed. She scrambled to her feet and, giggling, ran out of the room.

Luke shook his head as he scooped up the playing pieces and dumped them into their box. Females. What man would ever figure them out? They could be unpredictable. Unfathomable. And completely irresistible.

He rose to his feet, the Candyland box under his arm. It was time he claimed a female of his own. With Gloria's acceptance of his invitation and his aunt's agreement to undertake the arrangements for the gathering, everything was in place.

The family barbecue would be Real Lady Test Number One. It would serve several purposes. He would see how she conducted herself in a large social gathering, casual though it would be. He would observe how well she got along with his family. He could watch her interaction with children— there were about twenty of them of various ages.

Luke strode through the house into his study, where he laid out his bank statements and checkbook. As he went through the process of reconciling the accounts, he discovered a check missing. Or was it missing? Maybe he'd just messed up on the numbers he'd entered. What with all the work on the Blue Bonnet project and his preoccupation with Gloria there had probably been plenty of room for error. He decided to balance that account another evening. Right now he had Real Lady Test Number One to think about. It would tell him if he should proceed with his courtship of Gloria Hamilton.

This was one Cahill who was *not* going to take a bimbo bride.

Gloria pulled her old sedan into the garage of her neat little two-story house in one of Tidewater's renovated Victorian neighborhoods. Retired people and young couples lived in the modest, well-kept residences lining the streets.

Today had been more hectic than usual, with a Houston client needing to reschedule an appointment from later in the week to today, and another client arriving late. Alice had been her usual champion self and had stayed late to finish the mailer that Gloria had designed to increase business.

The keys on her ring jingled as she unlocked the door from the garage into the kitchen.

"Hamlet," she called, "I'm home."

"*R-r-r-rawk!* Welcome home! Welcome home!"

Gloria tossed her purse and keys onto the kitchen table and walked into the living room to the bird cage attached to a floor stand. "Pretty boy," she crooned to the gold-and-green sun conure. This member of the parakeet family looked like a small macaw.

The bird scrutinized her with black beady eyes, turning his head this way and that. "Hamlet's a pretty boy," he muttered. He ruffled his feathers and shook. Just as quickly, he laid his feathers smoothly back in place.

Gloria offered Hamlet a bit of sweet apple. He edged over to it on his bar, then, with his beak, daintily extracted the tidbit from between her fingers. He anchored it between the toes of one foot, then began gnawing at the morsel.

She watched Hamlet for a minute, then sighed. Is this what her life had come to? Being welcomed home by a conure? Not that he wasn't a fine figure of a conure and a delightful companion, she hastily amended her thought, feeling like a traitor. But...he *was* a bird. Not a husband. Not a daughter or a son. A little bitty bird.

She turned away from the cage to trudge to her bedroom, where she stripped off her suit and blouse and draped the garments over the back of a chair so she wouldn't forget to pick them up to take to the dry cleaners tomorrow. From a drawer in her highboy, she withdrew a pair of comfortable, if ratty-looking, shorts and a cutoff T-shirt. Quickly she plucked the pins from her hair, which she allowed to tumble to her shoulders. Had she given up on her dreams of having a real family? she wondered as she absently massaged her scalp. Had she allowed Charles to steal those dreams away from her, along with her trust?

She slipped her bare feet into a pair of brightly colored zoris, then went to the kitchen, the flip-flops slapping softly against the soles of her feet. The freezer compartment of her refrigerator yielded a frozen Italian dinner. A stint in the microwave oven changed the icy package into what would pass for a meal tonight, as similar packages had the nights before.

Stoically, Gloria forked down the concoction. She considered herself a pretty good chef, but she despised cooking for one. The beloved skills and rituals of cookery seemed to require a larger audience. Besides, she told herself once again, she really didn't have the time for all that stuff.

As she mechanically chewed and swallowed, her thoughts drifted to Luke Cahill. Now there was a man to start a woman's fantasies rolling. Tall, gorgeous, devilish, yet... kind. She'd witnessed him take the blame for Mrs. Gilder's incredible flying hen. The poor woman had looked ready to cry, but he'd drawn the class's attention to himself. Then, while Gloria had placed her students' attention squarely back where it should be—on their own skills—he had quietly worked with Mrs. Gilder until the woman was slicing away at his crisp game hen as if she'd been born to it. Oh, Gloria knew she shouldn't have let him usurp her role as instructor, but not only was he fascinating to watch, Mrs. Gilder seemed more comfortable with him, what with all his rakish teasing and jollying her along. Really, if the man ever set himself up as an etiquette-and-protocol teacher, Gloria suspected he would give her some very stiff competition. But, in the end, Mrs. Gilder had learned what she'd come there to learn, and so had all the other clients. As for Luke

Cahill...well, that had to be the most expensive pickup technique she'd ever seen. He'd paid over a hundred dollars for the opportunity to ask her to his family's barbecue because he clearly needed no coaching in dining skills.

As she went to the sink and rinsed out the plastic tray, then stuck it in the dishwasher, Gloria had to admit she was more than a little flattered.

On top of that, the man was trying to make good on his apology. In the past week since his invitation to the barbecue, she hadn't caught him once ogling her derriere as they entered the Grimble Building and rode the elevator up to their respective floors. Of course, they had shared one or two intense gazes. Even now, her pulse fluttered as she remembered his compelling blue eyes. Oh, dear, how they could play havoc with a woman's good sense. Gloria picked up a magazine and fanned her suddenly flushed face. Well, after this barbecue, Luke Cahill would realize that they really weren't suited, and that would be that.

Quickly Gloria squashed a twinge of disappointment. They *weren't* suited, and she'd best remember that. She preferred a calm, peaceful life. Mr. Cahill was entirely too exotic. He definitely wasn't the man for her.

Luke was whistling a cheerful tune when he entered his office the next morning. "Morning, Claire," he said, and continued with his melody, ignoring Claire's surprised expression.

"Good morning, Mr. Cahill."

She followed him into his office, steno pad in one hand, pink telephone messages in the other. Absently she switched on the coffeemaker on a side table. "You're awfully cheerful this morning. Did you win the lottery?"

He set his briefcase on the credenza, then hung his jacket in the concealed closet. "Nope."

Claire came to stand in front of his desk. "Then what?"

Luke smiled. "Things just seem to be going my way, that's all."

She nodded as if accepting that his answer would not get more specific than that, then handed him his messages.

Looking down at her steno pad, she began going down her list, reminding him of important appointments, of phone calls he needed to return or should expect to receive, and of his luncheon meeting with the parties involved in the development of the industrial park that Texas Gulf Properties was overseeing. That done, she left, closing his door behind her.

The familiar chug of the coffeemaker started up as Luke unpacked files and papers from his briefcase. The scent of freshly brewed coffee perfumed the air. Outside his window, white clouds studded the azure sky over the Gulf. Oh, yes, it was going to be a great day. He'd taken the first step toward finding the right woman.

Gloria. Even her name sent anticipation curling through him. Memories of her voice, of her laughter, of her mesmerizing yet somehow hesitant gaze wound around him like an ensnaring web.

He hoped she passed the tests.

His intercom buzzed, and he punched the button. "Yes?"

"Mr. Cahill, there's a Ms. Hamilton here to see you. She doesn't have an appointment—"

"Thank you, Claire. I'll see Ms. Hamilton." Luke rapidly strode across his office into the anteroom.

There she stood, next to Claire's desk, as gorgeous and as proper as usual. He briefly noticed her dark blue suit and white blouse, studiously keeping his gaze from lingering even for a second on taboo areas. Then he focused on her lovely face. Had he noticed the long length of her eyelashes before? Or the fact that her upper lip was just slightly fuller than her lower one?

She cleared her throat, and he realized he'd been staring. He concealed his chagrin with a smooth "Ms. Hamilton, please come in." He stood back to allow her to enter ahead of him. As she passed him, he noticed the jeweler's box in her hand.

He closed the door behind him, and she turned to face him.

"When I threatened to report you to the management of this building," she said, "I had no idea that *you* were the management. It wasn't until I called up here to find out where your office was that I learned of that fact." Her lips curved in a faint smile.

He gestured to one of the upholstered chairs in the conversation area. "Please, won't you sit down?"

"No, thank you. I only came to give you this." She held out the box. "You forgot to take it from me last week."

He made no move to take the silk-covered container from her. "No, I didn't. I very carefully selected that charm just for you. I want you to keep it."

She set the box on the corner of his massive desk. "Thank you, but I really can't keep it."

"Why not?" He covered all but a few steps of the distance between them. "Don't you like it?"

Gloria looked up at him, and he felt the impact of her direct gaze. It tugged at him, compelling him closer, drawing him in, until all he could see were sweet, intoxicating sherry brown pools.

"That has nothing to do with my returning it to you," she said.

Her statement served to break the spell, and he took an easier breath. "You haven't answered my question."

She frowned down at the box. "All right. I think the charm is adorable, but—"

"And so appropriate, don't you think?"

The corners of her luscious mouth twitched up. "Well, perhaps."

"Then keep it. Please."

Gloria shook her head. "No, really. I can't. It wouldn't be right."

Luke sighed. Oh, well. It was a minor setback only. "Okay, you win for now. But our date is still on, right? Next Saturday afternoon?"

She smiled. "Yes. Our date is on."

"Good. I'll pick you up at twelve."

"Wouldn't it be more sensible for me just to go to your house?"

"Maybe. But I'll still pick you up at twelve."

He walked with her toward his office door. Valiantly he resisted the temptation to pull her into his arms and kiss her pretty mouth. It would be soft and moist. He'd hold her close... Luke hastily dropped that dangerous line of thought when his body tightened with anticipation. He opened the door and escorted her out.

To his relief, Claire wasn't at her desk. "I hope you've been noticing that I don't follow you anymore?"

Gloria laughed, and the husky alto curled through him until he found he was smiling, too. "Yes," she admitted, "I've noticed. And I appreciate your restraint."

"I just want credit to go where it's due."

"Ah." Her eyes gleamed with humor.

Just as she turned to go, a stylishly groomed woman entered the reception area from one of the architects' offices. She wore a flashy couturier dress—nothing unusual, considering Texas Gulf Architects, a division of TGP, was the most prestigious architectural firm in Tidewater. What was unusual was the way the woman gave Gloria the once-over, then smiled an unpleasant, gloating smile.

Gloria paled, but drew herself up to regard Ms. Designer Dress with cool hauteur. Neither woman spoke. Without so much as a pause in her hip-dislocating stride, Ms. Designer Dress sailed through the door and out of the offices of Texas Gulf Properties. A second later, Luke heard the bell in the corridor that indicated the elevator's arrival.

When he turned back to Gloria, she was still deathly pale. "Are you all right?" he asked, then wanted to kick himself. Of course she wasn't all right. Any idiot could see that. "C'mon," he coaxed, trying to navigate her over to a waiting-room chair.

Easing out of his clasp, Gloria tossed him a quick, overbright smile. "I'm fine. Really." She walked to the twin mahogany doors that led out of TGP into the corridor. "I must be getting back. Alice will think I've gotten lost." Without another word, she glided out of the office.

She was good, Luke thought. Very good. Of course, someone who'd grown up in embassies around the world would be skilled at covering her feelings. But skill, it seemed, could not disguise the pallor of shock.

He stabbed out the interoffice number of the chief residential architect. "Pam, did you just finish an appointment with a blonde in an orange dress?"

"Suzette Elliot," Pam said promptly in answer to the question. "Mr. and Mrs. Elliot have recently moved here from Houston."

Elliot. Luke frowned. Why did that name ring a bell? "What's his first name?"

"Let's see here." Paper rustled. "Charles," Pam said.

After Luke thanked the architect and hung up, he reached for Ramsey's report on Gloria to confirm his suspicion. He reread the details of her marriage and how it had ended. Once again, he seethed at how Charles had cheated on her and how she'd discovered him having sex with his secretary on his desk. Anger expanded in Luke's chest when he saw the name of the secretary.

Suzette. The smirking creature in the gaudy designer dress was the woman Charles had been caught with. She'd become the second Mrs. Charles Elliot.

A peculiar desire to protect Gloria rose up in Luke with tidal force. He wanted to keep hurt and humiliation from touching her. He scarcely knew the woman, he reasoned, but that didn't seem to matter. Defying all logic, something inside him responded to her. It had from the moment he'd laid eyes on her.

It was that very reaction that troubled him. He had the ever-present examples of his father and his brother to remind him that Cahills and cat-around women were just naturally attracted. Was there a hidden side to Gloria that he just hadn't discovered yet? A . . . bimbo side? Could she be a floozy in lady's clothing? Luke's jaw tightened. Before he made any commitments, he'd damn sure find out.

Chapter Four

Gloria frowned as she studied herself in the full-length mirror in her bedroom. Were lightweight denim jeans and a matching shirt embellished with gold piping and gold buttons suitable for Luke's barbecue? For the first time in years, Gloria experienced uncertainty in selecting the right clothes for an occasion. The outfit seemed so...well... *casual*.

For a barbecue? A Texas barbecue at that? Why, where were her pointy-toed, reptile-skin cowboy boots? A genuine Stetson hat with a colorful feather band around the crown? She envied that flash and dazzle so many Texans possessed, along with their brash, good-humored confidence that allowed them to carry it all off without a moment of concern. Restraint had been the byword in clothing when Gloria had been learning the do's and don'ts of dressing. Life in embassies in remote, unstable nations had led the diplomats and their families to exercise caution in their attire as well as in their actions. She remembered her mother repeating the ancient Greek adage time and again: Simplicity is the mother of beauty. Gloria sighed. Sometimes it wasn't nearly as much fun as "More is better."

Well, these days she didn't have to worry about civil wars or military juntas. Turning away from the mirror, she decided to get wild and took from her closet a pair of red flats. Then she put on some bold gold earrings and braided her hair in a single, thick French braid, secured by an elastic band adorned with red wooden beads. Back at the mirror, she slicked on a bright red lipstick. A single gold bangle bracelet finished the picture. There. She didn't look flashy, but maybe no one would mistake her for a wallflower, either.

As she made her way downstairs, she took a deep, calming breath. For the past two weeks, she'd been infected with an excitement inappropriate to the occasion. After all, by going to the Cahill clan's barbecue with him, she would be allowing Luke to see for himself that she and he simply did not suit. He was used to being around beautiful people and was inclined to be a bit unpredictable, a quality she found disturbing. Tradition and method, those were her keynotes. They kept her in control of her life.

She heard a knock on the door and her stomach tightened.

"*R-r-r-awk!* Who is it? Who is it?" Rapeling down his stand's pole with his talons, Hamlet made it to the ceramic tiled floor and waddled halfway down the entry hall toward the door before Gloria recovered. "Who is it?" the bird demanded loudly, waddling faster when he saw Gloria, as if to beat her to the door.

As Gloria caught up with him, she heard a deep, masculine voice from outside say hesitantly, "It's Luke Cahill."

She couldn't suppress the laughter that bubbled up, cracking through and dispelling her nervousness. Quickly she placed her hand in front of Hamlet, and he obediently climbed on to perch. She opened the door.

Luke stood on her porch, tall, golden and utterly, breathtakingly male. Gloria's laughter died on her lips. His light blue, cotton-knit T-shirt revealed broad shoulders and strong arms. His wear-softened jeans hugged long legs and— Realizing where her gaze was headed, she tore it away, only to collide with Luke's.

She read amusement in the depths of his azure eyes and embarrassed warmth crawled up her neck to pound in her face. He knew.

The corners of his mouth curled up, but to her surprise he made no comment on her almost ogling. Instead, he nodded his head at Hamlet, who was busy cleaning one foot.

"Is this the sentry?" Luke asked.

As if realizing he was under discussion, the conure cocked his head, eyeing the newcomer.

"Yes...well... Some people get a gaggle of geese. I have Hamlet. He's a sun conure." She realized they were still standing on the porch, and she stepped aside, inviting Luke in with a sweep of her free hand. As he walked by, her gaze dropped to the tight, hard curve of a superb male backside outlined by his jeans. Guilt warmed her cheeks, and she forced herself to look farther down to see what kind of shoes he wore, as if to justify the direction in which she'd looked.

Boots. He wore Western boots. And not new ones, either, though they were well cared for. She knew he lived on a ranch outside of town—who in Tidewater hadn't heard of White Oaks? Until now, though, she'd never really pictured Luke in anything other than a tailored business suit.

Oh, what she'd been missing.

Determined not to get caught ogling, Gloria closed the door behind them and walked over to the large cage that hung next to Hamlet's unrestricted perch. She tried to put the bird inside.

"No, no, no!" he cried, grabbing the bars in the door with his feet and bracing himself against them, like a stubborn child refusing to be banished to his room.

"*No* is his favorite word," she explained, trying unsuccessfully to maneuver the resistant conure through the small opening.

"I'd say ol' Hamlet there has strong feelings about going into his cage," Luke said, watching with interest.

"No, no, no!"

Slightly embarrassed at Hamlet's behavior in front of a guest, Gloria sighed as she drew the conure away from the cage and smoothed his ruffled emerald and yellow feathers with the back of her fingers. "I'm afraid he wants to check you out. He likes to check out all visitors. And of course you have to tell him what a p-r-e-t-t-y b-o-y," she spelled out, "he is."

The corners of Luke's mouth quirked up. "He's not going to try to frisk me or anything, is he?"

Despite her self-conscious nervousness, Gloria couldn't help but smile. "Let's just say he's never done it before."

"Okay. I'm game. What do I have to do?"

"Just stand very still and speak softly to him. And, of course, tell him . . . you know."

Luke nodded, then stood perfectly still. Gloria approached him slowly, uncertain if her concern was for Hamlet's sake, or for hers. Good heavens, this man was tall. And—and...well...intimidating. The sheer size and power of him set her heart hammering. Until she noticed the uncertain, yet expectant expression on his face as he watched Hamlet riding on her hand. She stifled a giggle. Luke Cahill, the business lion of three counties, a towering, lean, hard-muscled giant of a man, was allowing himself to be checked out by a spoiled pet bird.

She lifted her hand until Hamlet sat in front of Luke's face, keeping a safe distance between them. So intent was she on maintaining that distance, watching for the conure's reaction, that the feel of a large, warm hand closing around hers, steadying it, startled her. She shot Luke a wide-eyed look, but he continued to regard Hamlet, who studied him, cocking his head this way and that, muttering to himself in small bird noises.

Gloria found it difficult to concentrate on what was taking place between bird and man while the feel of strong, masculine fingers around hers heated her skin. The heat spread down her arm to the rest of her body, leaving her feeling flushed and scattered.

Taking a deep breath, she focused with a will. Luke's hand *was* steadying, if not entirely necessary.

"Pretty boy," Luke said, and from the bloom of crimson color on his neck, Gloria guessed he felt silly saying it.

Hamlet tilted his head as if listening.

"Pretty boy," Luke repeated, this time with more animation. "Pretty boy." In fact, Luke's deep, drawling baritone was definitely taking on a crooning cadence. "Hamlet's a pretty boy."

Hamlet preened. "Hamlet's a pretty boy," he agreed. Gloria felt the bird's weight shift on her hand as he stretched to examine the large face in front of him. "To be or not to be."

A wide smile curved Luke's sensual mouth, revealing straight white teeth. "To be or not to be," he parroted.

Luke's hand guided Gloria's fractionally closer.

Immediately, Hamlet nuzzled Luke's nose. "Pretty boy," the bird murmured as if complimenting the man. Silently, Gloria agreed. Luke was most assuredly good to look at.

Hamlet "kissed" Luke's cheek, and Luke in turn gently stroked the smooth, brilliant feathers.

To Gloria's surprise, Hamlet hopped off her hand onto Luke's shoulder and began nuzzling Luke's ear. "I've never seen him do that before," she said. "He's never left my hand."

"Didn't I tell you? I'm irresistible to conures," Luke teased.

Gloria laughed. "So I see."

Luke tried to focus his eyes on Hamlet, who was now snuggled up against his ear, making Luke go slightly cross-eyed. "Are you sure Hamlet here isn't really a Hamletta?"

"He might be. He just flew into my garage one day and stayed. I've never tried to—" she coughed, her throat suddenly dry "—to check him." At that instant, she realized Luke had not released her. She couldn't help but stare at his hand, fascinated by its size and strength. If he wanted to, he could crush her hand like a walnut. Somehow, she couldn't imagine that large palm and those long, blunt-ended fingers with their clean, short-clipped nails doing anything of the sort, but she could imagine them signing papers, gentling one of the famous Cahill quarter horses, or…tenderly stroking a woman.

As that last, vivid image passed through her mind, Gloria quickly glanced up at Luke—to find him studying her.

Her cheeks grew warm. Oh, where did all her years of training, of social polish go when she was around this man? It was ridiculous. He wasn't even her type. She didn't *want* someone who made her blush, someone who made her forget the elegant manners she'd studied so hard to learn. Someone for whom her traitorous conure deserted her.

Luke winked at her.

Gloria blinked in confusion. "I...uh... Shouldn't we be going now?"

"I don't know," he said, a hidden smile warming his deep, Southern baritone. "I guess it depends on Hamlet."

Hamlet offered no comment as he nibbled on a strand of Luke's hair.

"Good night, sweet prince," Gloria said firmly, giving her bird a stern look.

"No, no, no!"

Luke lifted Gloria's hand to his shoulder where Hamlet perched. My, it was a broad, *solid* shoulder. She caught herself, and stealthily eased her fingers away from contact with him.

"Good night, sweet prince," Luke crooned, coaxing her hand closer to Hamlet, and Gloria choked down her laughter at the sight and sound of a towering, strapping Texan cajoling a reluctant conure off his shoulder.

Gloria could have sworn she heard Hamlet release a sigh of resignation as he hopped onto her hand. She almost released a sigh of her own when Luke let her hand go. Instead, she suppressed that inclination and carried her errant conure to his cage, then secured the door after him.

She picked up her purse, and Luke escorted her out of the house. He opened the passenger door of the sporty Mercedes Benz and she slid into the embrace of the leather seat. After shutting the door, he came around to the driver's side, where he folded into position behind the wheel.

I guess they just don't make sports cars for Texas-size men, she thought. Probably the only transportation with enough room to comfortably accommodate Luke Cahill's size was an eighteen-wheeler. Or a horse.

They chatted of nonconsequential matters as he maneuvered them through Saturday traffic, then out of town on the road that led to White Oaks. She'd been by the ranch several times. Set at least two miles back from the road, the columned mansion was surrounded by white-fenced paddocks and pastures, red-with-white-trim stables and barns that would have looked right at home in Virginia or Kentucky.

"How many guests do you expect?" she asked as he turned off the road onto the private drive that would take them to the house. The car passed beneath the white-painted wooden arch that bore the name of the ranch in neat black letters.

"This isn't a big shindig. Only family. You know, intimate. And neighbors, of course. Can't have a barbecue without having the neighbors over. They're practically family. So I'd say there'll be—oh—about a hundred people."

"A hundred?" she echoed. Good grief, he counted nearly a hundred people as intimate family? There had been three members of her family, seven if you counted both sets of grandparents, eight when you added Alice. "How many neighbors do you expect?" She watched sleek young horses gambol in the pastures as she silently wished she'd had the opportunity to get to know her grandparents better before they had passed away. Distances between their homes in the States and the array of diplomatic outposts her father had been consigned to had made travel extensive, expensive and risky. She could count their visits on the fingers of one hand.

"Maybe twenty-five, counting their kids and dates."

"I see."

Luke glanced over at her. "My family is rather large, and geographically it's scattered, but we stay in touch. You don't invite one without inviting the other. Someone's feelings would get hurt. My grandfather had four wives and twenty kids."

"Four wives?"

Luke's mouth curved up in a crooked smile. "One at a time."

"A conventional man, I see. Death or divorce?"

"Oh, death, of course. He loved his wives."

"With twenty children, I'd say so."

Luke turned the leather-covered steering wheel, guiding the car around the side of the vast house. "Yeah, well. Those twenty children had kids, and now their kids are having kids."

"Which accounts for such a large family."

He eased into what was clearly a temporary parking lot. A very crowded parking lot. "No one else has had twenty kids. Mostly my uncles, aunts and cousins have settled for two or three."

Gloria's parents had settled for one.

"And then there's my brother, Josh. So far, there's only Poppy, but she's an angel."

"Do you have any other brothers or sisters?"

"Nope." Luke turned off the ignition and turned to her. "But Josh has always been enough. And he's given me a very special niece."

The interior of the car seemed smaller than ever with the full force of Luke's attention focused on Gloria. The man always radiated a potent energy that strummed against her senses, and now it intensified. His bright blue gaze seemed to dive right inside her, plucking at her most secret wishes, her most carnal desires, all kept wisely, chastely suppressed. Everyone had fantasies, she told herself with weakening resolve. Only fools ever considered realizing such silly, damning fancies. To do so would be to risk losing control.

But as she was drawn into Luke's gaze, a small, defiant part of her surfaced to challenge a lifetime of discipline. Would it be so terrible, relinquishing control? For a terrifying second? A breathless moment? A thrilling hour? What harm could be done?

The world tumbled upside down as she sat there in the car, leaning slightly closer to Luke. Vaguely she realized that he had moved toward her. Infinitesimally, her lips parted, drawing breath in the suddenly heated interior.

What harm? echoed that inner voice.

Great harm.

Realization washed in, driving back the crazy, renegade urge to give in to serendipity, to the magnetic attraction that drew her to Luke, as inappropriate as that attraction might be. They weren't suited.

She eased back, feeling foolish, flustered.

"What happened?" Luke asked, his voice low.

Gloria wanted to pretend nothing had happened. If he was any kind of gentleman... "Happened?" she asked, then tensed as her voice went up too high to pass for a casual question.

He made no move to settle back in his seat, or even better, to get out of the car. "I was going to kiss you, and you pulled away."

An instant protest—a lie—flew to her lips. "I don't know what you mean." Guilty warmth poured into her face. Her color alone, she knew, would give her away. She'd always been a failure as a prevaricator. It was her one weakness as a social arbiter.

Luke leaned a little closer, and she discovered she couldn't get any farther back unless she opened the door. Instantly she rejected that alternative. She refused to run like a scared rabbit. She had her dignity to consider.

"You know exactly what I mean," he said, his hooded eyes roaming her face. "What I want to know is—" his lips almost touched hers "—why?"

She couldn't think, she couldn't breathe. All she could do was wish he'd stop talking and kiss her.

He made no move to cover that last fraction of distance between them. "Why?" he repeated softly, his warm breath caressing her lips.

Gloria struggled to produce a coherent thought. "Because...because..." Think. *Think.* "I don't believe we're suited."

She felt a distant uneasiness at the lazy smile that stole across his sensual mouth.

"Why?" he asked.

"Because you're unpredictable."

He moved fractionally closer. "Is that all?" he murmured.

"It's enough." Her protest was little more than formed air.

He gently brushed his lips across hers, and her eyes closed as the vibration of his touch shimmered through her. "We'll see," he whispered.

His mouth moved on hers in an electrifyingly sweet kiss that robbed her of her remaining gasp of breath and sent her center of gravity whirling into oblivion. Too soon, he lifted his head. She wanted to object, but she was still filled with a rolling giddiness that made speech impossible. He drew his fingertips softly down the side of her cheek. "We'll see."

Gloria swallowed hard. Oh, yes, he would see. Here was a man who enjoyed the stimulation and challenge of the unforetellable, the unpredictable. A man used to excitement. She, as he would discover all too soon, was totally, utterly predictable. She, Gloria By-The-Book Hamilton, was a veritable icon of convention. So she best not grow addicted to that enchanted-forest kiss of his.

Luke studied her for a moment, and she summoned a smile for him. Suddenly his handsome face lit with a smile of his own. "Well, let's party."

And as he came around to open Gloria's door and offered her his hand to assist her out, she stepped into a familiar situation. Voices and laughter drifted across the parking lot. A social gathering. Oh, she was good at this. She knew all the little graces and courtesies to smooth the way for her and those around her. No one would ever feel uncomfortable around her.

No one's heart would pound. No one's blood would course quickly through his veins.

Her pleasant smile remained in place as she firmly told herself pounding hearts and coursing, heated blood were unreliable. Uncontrollable. Not what she wanted at all. She'd do well to remember that.

A country and western band struck up a tune as Luke escorted her through a gate in a tall viburnum hedge. Verdant lawn formed a carpet upon which had been placed long ta-

bles with bright red, yellow and blue tablecloths and folding chairs. Fragrant smoke furled out from the edges of an
enormous black barbecue grill, but hamburgers had never
smelled that sweet and spicy. The big man wearing the white
apron over his Western shirt and jeans, a Stetson on his
head, opened the cover and basted with a thick red sauce the
two haunches of beef revolving slowly on the rotisserie.
Several yards away from the barbecue stood colorfully gar-
landed steam tables piled with food. There was a dessert table, a beverage table complete with cut-glass punch bowl,
and the inevitable well-stocked bar. On a temporary stage
erected some distance from the eating area, the band played
a rousing Texas two-step, and four couples were scuffing
across the wooden boards that had been laid down to serve
as a dance floor.

Luke had been right. There were at least a hundred people here. Most of the crowd were adults, but the giggles and
laughter of children were audible as several chased through
the eating area, to disappear around the other side of the
house.

Odd. As Gloria's eyes expertly assessed the gathering, she
noticed an unusual number of women with too much cleav-
age and thigh exposed. So many of them wore short, tight,
spandex dresses that it was practically a uniform. Heavily
made-up eyes. Bright, pouty lips. Jeez, it looked like bimbos on parade.

She put aside the puzzle as Luke guided her across the
lawn, threading their way through the crowd. Pausing only
for a word of greeting here, a warm handshake there, Luke
promised to come back to make introductions as soon as
Gloria met Aunt Maudie. Gradually, Gloria began to envi-
sion Luke's aunt as some imperial dowager, holding court
from her high-backed throne, while her subjects came to
genuflect before her. Well, Gloria thought, licking dry lips,
because of her father's postings, she'd been introduced to
crowned heads before—usually shortly before those heads
were removed by an angry citizenry in revolt—so she wasn't
going to be intimidated by some Gulf Coast family matri-
arch.

To her relief, when Luke finally tracked Aunt Maudie down, that lady was not enthroned, nor surrounded by her obsequious minions, but rather seated in a lawn chair, with a baby on her lap and a shrieking, giggling toddler wrestling with a leggy golden Labrador retriever puppy at her feet. Other women encircled the painted aluminum table, many holding children or watching them playing on the ground near their feet. Some of the women were obviously pregnant. One of them had long, flat-black hair, too much makeup and a very short, very tight skirt. It flashed through Gloria's mind that maybe there was a bimbo maternity-wear shop somewhere in Tidewater. A few husbands lolled in their chairs, watching the party, yet keeping half an eye on the kids.

Slim and tall, in her mid-sixties, with blue eyes and stylishly cut silver gray hair, Maudie Cahill Forysth smiled warmly up at Gloria and clasped her hand with a reassuring little squeeze. "I'm so glad you could make it to our barbecue. It isn't often that I get to meet a friend of Luke's."

"Yeah, he hasn't brought a girl home to meet the family since his sweetie, Barbara Tuttle. You know, that waitress from that nudie place down on Highway—*uumph!*" The speaker, one of the husbands, was promptly silenced when the woman next to him plunked a large toddler down in his lap. He gave the woman an aggrieved look, and from the narrow-eyed warning he received in return, Gloria guessed her to be his wife.

"Ancient history," another of the women said.

Ms. Flat-Black Hair snapped her gum. "Yeah, well, I'll bet she's havin' a helluva lot more fun than I am at this *party.*" She hoisted herself out of the chair and lumbered off toward the activity.

Out of the corner of her eye, Gloria noticed the thundercloud of Luke's face. The other men shifted in their seats. The women glanced uncomfortably at one another.

Gloria politely ignored the incident. "I'm so glad Luke invited me. I've never been to a family gathering of this size before, and I'm finding it very exciting. I come from a very small family, you see, so this is an adventure for me."

Maudie and the others laughed. "Gloria," Luke's aunt said, her eyes twinkling, "it's an adventure for all of us. When life seems to be getting a little dull, why, we just all get together, eat and dance."

Gloria smiled. "Sounds like a good plan to me."

Maudie made the rest of the introductions around the table. Gloria met several of Luke's cousins and their children.

"Come back and see me," Maudie said softly with a smile. She gave Gloria's hand another little squeeze before Luke swept her off to the food tables.

There they encountered his younger brother, Josh, whose photo she'd recently seen in the newspaper, and Luke's father, Daniel Cahill, senior business lion. He had to be. According to the newspapers and the guy who worked in the sandwich shop, Daniel Cahill was still paying three of his five ex-wives alimony. A lot of alimony. Two of the five had remarried, for which, she imagined, he was vastly thankful.

She felt as if she was being sized up by both Daniel and Josh—perfectly natural, she told herself, resisting the urge to squirm. Finally, Daniel excused himself and drifted away, full plate in one hand and a leggy blonde with eight-inch fingernails and a sprayed-on bodysuit in the other. Gloria watched as the woman tiptoe-minced away. Curious. Very curious. Was this the Texas version of *The Stepford Wives* taking place even as she watched?

Josh sat down with them at an empty picnic table. "Luke tells me that you both work in the same office building."

Gloria scooped some potato salad onto her fork. "Yes." Her gaze strayed toward Luke. She found the humor that lurked in the depths of his blue eyes, and she knew instinctively that he hadn't told his brother the exact circumstances of their first encounter. "We, uh, met on the elevator."

"Is that so? On the elevator? Well, that's interesting. Usually people *stop* talking on elevators." Josh took a bite from his corn on the cob, studying her all the while.

"It was sort of an unusual set of circumstances," she said smoothly, noticing the edges of Luke's ears were turning bright pink. The adorable man was blushing!

"Unusual?" Josh asked. "In what way?"

She smiled at Luke's brother. "Unusual in that people usually do *stop* talking on elevators. I...introduced myself."

"You did? Well, well. This really is the nineties."

"And if someone wants to live to see the new millennium, he'd better cut out the interrogation," Luke said bluntly. "This is a party, Josh, not the Spanish Inquisition."

"My, someone is testy," Josh said. "I'm only showing a brother's natural curiosity. Gloria will tell me if she thinks I'm getting too nosy, won't you, Gloria?"

Gloria smiled sweetly. "You're getting too nosy, Josh."

"Oh."

A small hand and thin, childish arm slipped around Josh's neck. "Daddy, can I eat with you and Uncle Luke?" whispered the little blond girl who clung to Josh's side.

The radiant tenderness that shone in Josh's face as he looked at his child touched something deep inside Gloria. She glanced at Luke, and to her surprise, she witnessed a soft affection in his handsome face that rivaled Josh's. This fortunate child was cherished by the two men. In her own bitter experience, men wrapped themselves up in their careers until their wives ceased to be companions and partners. Instead, they faded into extensions of the office staff and head housekeeper, and their children almost entirely vanished.

She had wanted a family. Children. Charles had wanted...other things. For a while, she had been one of those things. His hostess. When her dull, eager, *blind* usefulness had worn out, she'd been replaced. The hollow place in Gloria ached, and she struggled to crush the painful envy that threatened to grow.

Josh lifted his daughter up and onto the picnic bench. "Where's your food, Poppy?"

"Granddaddy's bringing it," she said. She regarded Gloria with large green eyes and leaned back against her father.

"Gloria, I'd like to introduce Josh's daughter, Poppy. Poppy, this is my friend, Ms. Hamilton."

"How do you do, Poppy?" Gloria asked with an encouraging smile.

Poppy regarded Gloria in silence with wide, watchful eyes.

Josh gently nudged his daughter. "What do you say to Ms. Hamilton?" he asked softly.

A small thumb popped into Poppy's mouth, and from the motion of her cheeks, Gloria knew the child was sucking on it. The girl looked to be about five or six—too old to be sucking her thumb. Something wasn't right in Poppy's life.

Before Josh could speak to the child again, Daniel Cahill arrived at their table with a plate of food in each hand. "So this is where the butterfly has flown," he exclaimed in mock astonishment, and the thumb exited Poppy's mouth as she giggled.

Daniel sat down on the other side of his granddaughter, across the table from Luke and Gloria.

Gloria studied the strong family resemblance between the four Cahills sitting around her. Even Poppy bore the family stamp of fair coloring and beauty. The child could have beat out the Softy Tissue girl any day. Of course, the beauty didn't come only from the men's side of the family. Gloria casually gazed around her at all the gorgeous women whose voluptuous bodies were so evidently displayed by low necklines and skimpy skirts and shorts and breath-defyingly tight jeans.

It was enough to make a more conservative woman feel downright dowdy.

"Luke tells us you work in the Grimble Building, Gloria," Daniel Cahill said. "Hamilton Consulting, right?"

She smiled, secretly pleased that Luke had talked of her to his family. "Yes, sir."

Daniel grimaced. "Oh, please, we can do away with the sir, can't we? It makes me feel my age. Call me Daniel."

"All right."

"Still, it's good to see courtesy isn't dead in some areas of the country. When I was a boy—"

"There you are! There's my little grandbaby!" a woman in her late fifties exclaimed. Her long, artfully tousled, platinum blond hair brushed bare shoulders that had long ago passed that one-tan-too-many stage, and her skin had taken on the look and texture of old leather. Her off-the-shoulder peasant blouse might have worked well on one of the many younger, well-endowed females, but it revealed too clearly that time and gravity had not been kind to this woman, whoever she was. Gold lamé toreador pants hugged hips and legs that were still shapely. A column of gold-and-diamond bracelets sheathed each wrist.

Luke stiffened. Josh's expression went completely blank. Daniel's face darkened with wrath. He turned in his place to face her.

"What are you doing here, Lydia?" he said in a low, furious voice.

A tight smile curved Lydia's brightly colored and glossed lips. "I came to see my one and only grandbaby." She bent and picked up Poppy. "My, you're getting to be such a *big* girl. Look what Grammy brought you." She snapped her fingers, and a handsome, swarthy young man, whose dark chauffeur's uniform did not disguise his bodybuilder's physique, stepped up from behind her. Despite the heat of the day, over one arm was draped a woman's full-length sable coat. He presented a flat, rectangular package wrapped in gleaming gold foil and tied with a gold foil ribbon.

Hesitantly, Poppy took it from him. She turned questioning eyes toward her father, her uncle and her grandfather.

"Here, baby, Grammy's got to put you down now before her back goes out." Lydia tried to lower Poppy back onto the bench, but Josh held out his arms, and his daughter went scrambling to safe haven.

"Well, aren'tcha going to at least unwrap your present?" Lydia asked.

After a nod from her father, Poppy quietly tore away the wrapping. As she worked, Lydia looked at Luke.

"And just when are you going to get married, for God's sake?" she demanded. "Your younger brother's the only one giving me grandchildren. Of course, he's only given me one, but he'll get married again." She cast a venomous glance at Daniel. "Cahill men always do."

Steel glinted in Luke's eyes as he regarded his mother. "I'll marry," he said coldly, "when I find the right woman."

The corners of Lydia's overpainted mouth drew down. "Meaning one *not* like me."

"Precisely."

"Fat chance," she sneered. "You'll marry a woman exactly like me. All the Cahill men do. Just look at your brother."

"Bunnie is nothing like you," Josh said quietly.

"Look, Daddy," Poppy said as she opened a shiny black case to reveal a dark rainbow selection of lipsticks and eye shadows from an expensive cosmetics line. This was no child's toy with water-soluble colors.

"Oh, for cryin' out loud, Lydia," Daniel said in disgust. "Use your head. This is a woman's makeup kit."

"Why should she have to mess around with some cheap crap when she can have the real thing? I'd have killed to have something nice like that when I was a girl."

Josh snapped the case shut and handed it back to his mother. "I'm sorry, Mom, but she's just too young. Maybe you know someone who could use it."

"Like a needy ten-year-old," Luke said dryly.

Lydia angrily snatched the makeup kit from Josh's hand. She turned to glare at Gloria. "What about you? Do you want this?"

"Thank you, no. I'm afraid they aren't my colors." They were, actually, but Gloria had no intention of accepting the inappropriate gift. What grandmother gave such a young child fire-engine red lipstick and midnight blue eye shadow?

It sent the wrong message to the girl for one thing, not to mention the stains it would create if left in small hands.

Lydia's gaze raked over Gloria, who felt she'd just been judged and found wanting. "I see," Lydia said.

Without another word, she spun on her gold sandal heel and stalked off, the pumped-up chauffeur trailing behind her. The five of them at the table watched as she dropped the case into a trash receptacle.

Poppy started to sniffle. Her bottom lip quivered. "Why was Grammy mad?" she asked in a small, plaintive voice. "Why did she leave?"

As Josh and Daniel sought to comfort and explain, Luke looked at Gloria. "I'm sorry about that," he said. "I never intended for you to see my family quite so up close and personal."

"No?"

His wonderful mouth curved up in a crooked smile. "No. I only wanted you to see the good stuff."

As she gazed at him, at his summer blue eyes, his perfect, crooked nose, his irresistible mouth, Gloria felt herself drawn away from her everyday moorings. "Like what good stuff? In particular?"

"Like my aunt—"

Gloria nodded. "Definitely good stuff."

"And my niece, Poppy—"

"Okay. More good stuff."

"And my brother and father—"

"I'll give you that. Also good stuff."

He extended his arms to embrace the area. "And my family and my home."

"All right, all right, I concede," she said, laughing. "All good stuff except for a few awkward moments."

Luke released an exaggerated sigh. "Whew! You had me worried there for a minute." He brushed her hand where it rested on the bench between them. Her skin tingled where his fingers touched it.

"I do have one question," Gloria blurted nervously, then instantly wished she could take her words back.

Luke drew a forefinger over the top of her wrist.

She found it hard to think. This was ridiculous! The man had barely touched her with one finger, and she could hardly breathe. "Never mind." What could she say? What's with the bimbos on parade? That would go over like a snore in church.

"No, go on," he coaxed. "Ask me your question."

She glanced over at Daniel and Josh to find them occupied with Poppy. "I forgot," she lied. "I'm afraid the question just slipped away."

Luke just looked at her without saying anything, and Gloria devoutly wished the earth would open up and swallow her. She should never even have *thought* about asking.

"I think we all know what's piqued the lady's curiosity," Josh said, and Gloria looked up to discover Poppy gone and the full attention of Josh and Daniel focused on her conversation with Luke.

Where was a nice cozy rat hole to crawl into when you needed one? she thought. "No, really—"

"Tell her, son," Daniel urged, a note of resignation in his deep voice.

Luke sighed. "It's the curse of the bimbo bride."

Chapter Five

Gloria was still pondering the three men's theory of the bimbo bride curse as she crossed the lawn, coming back from a visit to the powder room. Luke, Josh and Daniel actually seemed to believe their own words, and she certainly couldn't deny the unusually large number of women at the barbecue who—at least in appearance—qualified for the description of "bimbo."

She heard her name called and turned to find Maudie waving her over. The other adults had wandered off, taking most of the children with them. Luke's aunt held a different baby now. A few youngsters sat on the grass near her lawn chair, Poppy among them.

"Come keep an old woman company for a while," Maudie said when Gloria strolled over. "I've been left alone to tend the nursery."

Gloria laughed at the idea of Maudie being an old woman. There was something timeless about that lady, something magnetic that drew even strangers to her in trust. Gloria sat down in the empty chair next to Maudie. Immediately, a toddler in grass-stained light blue overalls appeared, holding out his arms to indicate he wanted to be picked up. Without thinking, Gloria lifted him up onto her lap, where he snuggled back against her, chattering happily. Sitting here next to Maudie, it seemed only natural to be holding a child.

"Is Daniel your brother?" Gloria asked.

"Yes," Maudie said. "I moved back to White Oaks when my husband passed away ten years ago. Poppy and I are the only two females here now." She smiled down at the little girl, who smiled back, but there was a faint note of sadness in Maudie's voice.

Gloria stroked the fine brown hair of the tot in her lap. He seemed content to cuddle up in her arms. His unquestioning acceptance of her warmed a little corner of her heart.

"I just heard the strangest thing," she said, her gaze wandering toward a cluster of voluptuous, long-legged beauties, every one of them wearing skimpy, blatantly sexy clothing. The hot, bright summer sun glinted off diamonds and gold and platinum. She saw that more than one shapely jaw hammered away at a wad of chewing gum.

"I take it you've been told about the curse," Maudie said.

Gloria nodded. "It's one of the oddest notions." Yet, there was the evidence.

Another child found her way over to the "nursery." The little girl looked to be about four. She sat down on the grass next to Poppy and leaned back against Maudie's leg.

"The curse?"

Gloria looked at Maudie, feeling slightly foolish. "Yes."

The older woman sighed. "Well, I'm sure it has something to do with self-image, self-esteem, self-worth, high testosterone—something of the sort. But the fact is, the men in this family do seem to marry the more, uh, shall we say, *showy* young women." Maudie shrugged. "Unfortunately, more often than not, in two or three years—sometimes not that long—the marriages break up."

Gloria hesitated. "I met Lydia Cahill about an hour ago."

"Oh, dear. Is *she* here? I certainly didn't invite her."

"She gave Poppy a Ventru Cosmetics kit."

"For heaven's sake." Maudie shifted with agitation in her chair.

"Josh gave it back."

"Well, good for him. The last thing Poppy needs is expensive makeup."

"The colors were pretty," Poppy said. "Like my paints."

Gloria smiled at the girl. "Do you paint, Poppy?"

The child nodded.

"Why don't you go get some of the pictures you made, so Miss Hamilton can see them?" Maudie suggested.

"Oh, yes, Poppy," Gloria said. "I'd love to see your pictures."

"Okay." Poppy got up and skipped off to the house.

"She's very artistic," Maudie said, "and I assure you that it's not just the ravings of a biased great-aunt."

Gloria chuckled. "Great-aunts are supposed to be biased where their nieces and nephews are concerned."

"Poppy gets her talent from her mother, Bunnie. Now there was a marriage I was sorry to see break up. For a while it looked as if those two might lay the curse to rest. But their pride and their hot tempers finally got the better of them."

Back across the lawn came Poppy, her childish legs carrying her as fast as they could. She clutched large rectangles of thick paper, which she gave to her great-aunt, who turned them over to Gloria. Careful not to disturb the toddler dozing in her lap, Gloria held the papers out where she could get the full impact of the vibrant watercolors. The child showed talent, she thought. There was an untutored grace to the lines of the pictures, to the sweeping strokes of color.

"These are lovely, Poppy," Gloria told the youngster as she studied the vividly painted images. She could make out White Oaks, with its tall white columns and portico, surrounded by emerald fields. Poppy had even painted grazing horses and the wide-spreading oaks that dotted the pastures.

Poppy leaned her slender little body against Gloria's legs. Large, bright green eyes anxiously fixed on Gloria's face as one picture after another was examined. "You're a very gifted young lady," Gloria said sincerely, after she'd seen all the paintings. She selected the one of White Oaks. "You see,

I recognized this immediately. You've captured so many important details. The angle of these horses' necks tells me they're grazing. And see here? You've done the correct number of columns, and you've got the pediment just right over the portico. And the jasmine climbing up the side of the house. A lot of people would have missed that."

The six-year-old hung on Gloria's every word of praise, her chin resting on her small hands, her elbows poking into Gloria's thighs. "They would?"

Gloria nodded solemnly. "That's right. And look here, at this one you did of your uncle Luke's office building. I knew as soon as I saw it that this was the Grimble Building. There are many Victorian buildings that have been renovated on this street, but I knew which one it was because you've captured important details." She went on to point out the elements that had impressed her about the watercolor. Poppy's flushed pleasure warmed Gloria. She laid the papers on her lap and reached out with her one free hand to smooth back wisps of moonlight hair that had escaped the girl's braids. "You have a rare gift, little love."

The black-haired pregnant woman who had so ungraciously left the nursery area when Gloria had first arrived at White Oaks lumbered into the shade of the towering old tree, followed by two children, a boy and a girl, who looked to be about seven or eight. The woman lowered herself into the chair next to Gloria's.

"Can we get some ice cream?" the boy asked.

"Yes, but first see if anyone else would like some," the woman said.

"Aunt Maudie, would you like some ice cream?" the girl asked.

"No, thank you, dear. I'm too full of barbecue."

"Poppy, want some ice cream?" the boy inquired.

Poppy shook her head, her thick braids thumping back and forth against her shoulders.

"What do you say, Poppy?" Maudie firmly prompted.

"No, thank you, Bubba."

Bubba turned to Gloria. "Ma'am, would you like some ice cream?"

Pleased to see children being taught the courtesies, she smiled. "No, thank you, Bubba, but I appreciate your asking."

Bright color bloomed in his cheeks. "My pleasure, ma'am."

"Okay," the pregnant woman said. "But come right back."

The children skipped off toward the ice-cream wagon, located at the end of the food line.

"It's nice to see children learning manners," Gloria said.

The dark-haired woman smiled wearily. "Yeah, well, I'm trying. It's just me an' Emily Post against the barbarians."

"It looks as if you're winning."

"For the moment." The woman laid her head back against the back of the lawn chair and closed her eyes. Her skin seemed unusually pale.

A concerned frown touched Maudie's face as she studied the woman. "Tiffany, you're looking done in. Why don't you go lie down inside?"

The woman opened her eyes. "I'm okay, Maudie. Really. It's just that it's so hot, and I'm so big.... I get tired, that's all."

Maudie looked unconvinced. "If you change your mind, just go on into the yellow guest room. It'll give you some peace and quiet."

Tiffany smiled. "Thanks." The smiled faded, and the woman looked down at the mound of her stomach that now covered her lap. When she looked up, her gaze was directed at both Maudie and Gloria. "I want to apologize for earlier. I was out of line, being so rude. This is a great party, Maudie. Your parties always are. It's just... Well, I'm hot and cranky and miserable. I know that's no excuse, but... I'm sorry. Honestly I am."

Gloria gave Poppy a little hug with her one free arm. "Poppy, love, will you go get your aunt Tiffany a tall glass of nice cold lemonade, and then another glass with nothing but ice? Then, when you come back, we'll show her your wonderful paintings. I think they'll make her feel better, don't you?"

Her eyes shining, Poppy ran off to fetch the lemonade and ice. Maudie handed Gloria her sweet burden, so that now each of Gloria's arms was filled with a sleepy-eyed child.

"I'm going to get a wet washcloth to put the ice in," Maudie said, and went into the house.

"I imagine being outside in this hot weather is miserable for you," Gloria said to Tiffany. She introduced herself.

Tiffany offered her hand, and they shook. "Tiffany Cahill." She smiled, and Gloria realized that under all that makeup, and despite the vanishing pallor, Tiffany was younger—in her early twenties—than she appeared at first glance. "You're the lady who teaches manners, aren't you?"

Gloria felt a tug on her hair, and looked down into an alert pair of brown eyes. One toddler was no longer asleep. Suddenly wet warmth seeped onto her hand. "Uh-oh."

Tiffany grinned. "I recognize that sound."

"I need a diaper, fast." Gloria looked around for one, but saw none.

Levering herself out of her chair, Tiffany waddled over to an empty table and pulled back the colorful crepe-paper skirt to reveal boxes of diapers. "This is the changing table."

"Oh. I thought it was a refreshment table waiting for refreshments." Gloria handed over the still-slumbering infant to Maudie, who'd returned with the wet washcloth. Hurrying over to the changing table, Gloria made quick work of stripping off the soaked romper and diaper, and taping the squirming little boy into a dry one.

"I'm afraid Baby Bobby Joe got you," Tiffany said, holding the cooling cloth to her forehead with one hand and pointing to Gloria's lap with the other.

Gloria looked down to see a dark spot the size of a handprint on the right thigh of her denim jeans. Oh, great.

Tiffany went into the house and came back with another wet cloth. "I sprayed some carpet cleaner on it," she explained.

"Carpet cleaner?" Maudie and Gloria asked in unison, their eyebrows lifting.

"It's all I could find in a hurry."

Gloria shrugged. "Hey, it works on carpets. Why not denim? Thanks, Tiffany."

Tiffany took up the freshly changed child while Gloria scrubbed at the dark spot on her jeans. To Gloria's dismay, the spot foamed up white and grew in size. Well, if she wanted to prove to Luke that she wasn't his type, this was certainly the way to do it.

But, as she dipped a clean corner of the rag in a glass of water Poppy got for her, she discovered mixed emotions about that. She liked being with him. She even liked his family. And she certainly liked the way he kissed her.

As she blotted away the white foam, she told herself she was being foolish. What woman wouldn't like being with Luke? He was heart-in-your-throat handsome, funny, sizzlingly sexy...

And unpredictable.

She must not allow herself to forget that. Every week in the newspaper there was at least one account of how he had outwitted a business rival with some unexpected maneuver. Often there had been risk involved. He was a man who enjoyed risk, a man who enjoyed skating on the edge. Gloria blotted harder at the wet denim.

She'd lived too many years on the edge. The government and her father had been the risk takers then, but their stakes hadn't been just a piece of land, an industrial development or mineral rights. The pieces on their game boards had been human lives. Very real, very warm, very immediate humans to Gloria. The government and her father had not always won their moves. And the pawns often paid the true price with their blood.

Unclenching her fingers from around the cloth, she drew in a long, deep breath, easing the tension that had sprung into the muscles in her chest and shoulders. It was safer, much safer, to be cautious—even if it meant being dull.

When she took the freshly changed toddler back into her arms, his warmth and weight, his soft, happy chattering banished her tension. She smiled down at him, and he broke out into a wide, wet smile.

"Tiffany, come sit down," she said coaxingly.

As Tiffany awkwardly lowered herself into the lawn chair, Poppy gave her the lemonade and received grateful thanks.

Maudie settled in a chair on one side of Tiffany, while Gloria sat on the other side. Taking up the watercolors, Gloria began to show off Poppy's work, liberal with her praise. Poppy sat on the ground where she could see the paintings and hear what was being said, leaning her head back contentedly against Gloria's hip.

Luke found them that way.

When Gloria had not come back to the animated discussion of football, Luke had gone to search for her. When he spotted her at the nursery, Baby Bobby Joe was nestled in the curve of her arm as she showed off Poppy's watercolors. Maudie listened and smiled benignly, clearly enjoying Poppy's debut. Tiffany and her two kids studied the paintings as if they were going to be tested on what was being said. Poppy leaned trustingly against Gloria's side, drinking it all in, her thumb nowhere near her mouth.

Gloria seemed completely comfortable holding the small boy while praising a child's primitive artwork like a proud parent. Somehow she'd coaxed shy Poppy and grouchy Tiffany into relaxing. He thought Gloria looked like a twentieth-century Madonna.

Luke edged a little closer and saw a small, chubby fist entangled in Gloria's hair, and a smile floated up from the warm spot expanding in his chest. God, she was beautiful, sitting there, surrounded by children, by his family. Anyone would think that she'd been friends with these people for years, instead of just hours.

Out of the corner of his eye, he caught Maudie looking at him. She gave him a single nod, and he grinned. She approved of his choice.

As he walked over to the group, Luke felt an increased spring to his step. Gloria might well be The One. Lord knew there was strong chemistry between them. His blood heated just looking at her. But he couldn't allow that to cloud his judgment. It was exactly what had happened to the other men in his family, he was sure.

Gloria had gotten through to his shy little niece, who now leaned against her, hanging on her every word. The words he caught on the summer breeze were good ones, words that would strengthen Poppy's confidence. For that alone, he wanted to hug Gloria, to kiss her, and make his own babies with her. A feeling of satisfaction flowed up in him. He'd have to wait on making babies with her until she passed the rest of the tests and they settled things between them, but he could still hug and kiss her.

As he dropped down into the chair next to her and shot her a smile, he reminded himself that she still had reservations about him. Her manner had made that clear in the parking garage two weeks ago. True, she'd accepted his invitation to the barbecue, but that didn't mean everything was clear sailing. She'd require some patience and a light touch.

He reached over and smoothed a forefinger over the silken brown hair of the little boy she held. Bright eyes peered at him from over her shoulder.

He'd have a fine line to walk, Luke thought. He didn't want to lead her on with an all-out courtship as long as there was a possibility that things might not work. But keeping his hands off her would be hard. Damned hard.

It had taken all his willpower not to deepen their kiss in the car. He'd been almost crazy with the scent of her, the softness of her, the taste of her. He'd wanted to peel off her clothes and slip his hands over her flushed, warm body. His blood had pulsed hot and thick through his veins.

He sighed as he shifted uncomfortably in his chair. This quest for a Real Lady wasn't going to be easy. For one thing, a Real Lady would expect to be treated as such, and that's the way it should be, he hurried to reassure himself.

"What's wrong, Luke?" Gloria asked.

He blinked and looked around. Tiffany had gone, and Gloria was no longer holding the child. He caught sight of Poppy just as she and her two cousins disappeared into the house. Maudie still sat in her lawn chair, holding a baby.

"Wrong?" he echoed.

"You're scowling," Gloria observed.

"Oh."

"Maybe Luke has been waiting to ask you to dance," Maudie suggested.

Gloria turned expectant eyes toward him.

"That's right. I, uh, was just waiting for someone to come claim their kid so I could ask you."

"Well, they have, so you two young people run along now," Maudie commanded, as a woman came to fetch the child she cradled.

Luke looked at Gloria, waiting.

"Why, I'd be plumb tickled to dance with you," she said with a grin.

He grabbed her hand and headed in the direction of the dance area. Then he heard the band begin a rousing tune. "C'mon," he said. "We can't miss this. It's one of my favorites." They ran hand in hand to join the dancers.

Luke placed his palm at the small of Gloria's back and swept her into a jaunty Texas two-step. Her eyes sparkled, and her delectable mouth curved up in a wide smile just this side of laughter, revealing a glimpse of even white teeth. Roses bloomed in her cheeks, and her dark braid bounced against her shoulders. As he swirled her around the temporary dance floor, Luke felt like a boy with his best girl at a school dance. He raised his head and let loose a Rebel yell for the pure joy of it. Several other men followed suit, and as if infected with the same high spirits, the band stepped up the tempo of the music, challenging the dancers to keep up.

By the time Luke pulled his car into Gloria's driveway hours later, there had been many more dances, some just as fast, others slow and sensual. He and Gloria had scooped up ice-cream cones that had melted all too quickly, resulting in pink-tongued licks and sweet, cream-covered lips. Which had invited a quick, stolen kiss.

Luke turned off the ignition and came around to open Gloria's door, helping her out of the low-slung automobile.

He escorted her up the curving concrete walkway to the all-too-brightly lit front porch, his hand riding lightly at the small of her back.

She fiddled with her keys. "I had a lovely time," she said and smiled.

"Good." He was loath to remove his hand from her. It took self-restraint not to curl his fingers inward to feel her rounded muscles and the feminine dip in the center of her back before he dropped his hand to his side. "Now it's your turn."

Her fingers stilled on the keys. "My turn to what?"

He gave her his most winning smile. "Well, I provided a barbecue today. Now it's your turn to pick the time and place. You really can't do the barbecue thing. We've already done that. What about a picnic?" He pretended to consider his own suggestion for a moment. "No. Too hot outside. A movie? No. Too noisy inside." He brightened. "I've got it! The perfect solution."

"Don't tell me. Let me guess," she said, the corners of her mouth twitching. "You'd like to do something somewhere quiet inside."

"Now here's a woman who knows how to read a man's mind," he said, his voice dropping to a more intimate level. He moved closer.

Her keys rattled between her fingers. "That's something I'd never even try to do."

He lifted an eyebrow. "Why not? Reading a man's mind could be very convenient."

"*Convenient* isn't the word I would have chosen."

"No? What word would you have used?"

"Scary."

Luke laughed. "Scary? You think men are scary?"

Amusement shone in her eyes. "No. I think men are really aliens from another world. The prospect of delving into a mind wired so differently from mine is downright scary."

"An alien. Gee, thanks."

"Well," she said, humor bubbling beneath the surface of her voice, "you have to admit there are some very basic differences between the sexes."

"Oh, yeah." His lips curved up. "Very basic."

Her keys jingled.

"Still," he said, "you'll have to agree that there are certain basic things we all have in common." Even in the harsh porch light, she was lovely. Her dark hair framed her fair, oval face. He found himself fascinated with her large brown eyes. They appeared opaque or as translucent as sherry in a glass, depending on the way she turned her head.

"Such as?"

"The fear of falling. The drive to reproduce. The—need—to—eat." He looked at her hopefully.

She smiled. "Ah. I see. Is this, perchance, your way of saying you'd like me to invite you to dinner?"

"Are you sure you don't read minds?"

"Let's just say I only need to be hit over the head with your subtlety once."

He moved closer still. It was all he could do not to capture her in his arms. He could feel the warmth of her body along his. Her fingers twitched around her keys, and he gently eased them out of her hand.

"So what do you say?" he asked. "Have pity on a poor, starving fella."

She hesitated, and he found himself holding his breath. "Next Saturday at seven?" she finally asked. All of the amusement had gone out of her voice.

The weight that had been growing in his chest lifted like a helium balloon. "At seven on Saturday it is," he agreed, ridiculously pleased.

She looked away. "This is pointless, you know."

A chill bored into the middle of him. "It is?"

"We aren't suited. We're just too different from each other."

With the first two fingers of one hand set along her jaw, he brought her face toward him, and tipped up her chin so that her gaze met his. "We'll see," he murmured. Then he took her into his arms and kissed her.

Gloria felt the world go spinning as Luke set his lips to hers. Her heart leapt into a Texas two-step of its own as he took her bottom lip between his teeth and held it prisoner while his tongue slipped back and forth over it. Her brazen arms wended their way up his chest to twine around his neck. Of their own volition, her lips parted under his. Immediately he deepened the kiss. His tongue swept into her mouth like a conquering force pouring through a breached gate. It swirled over her teeth, traced the inside of her cheeks, then cunningly stroked her tongue, teasing and tempting her until her fingers inched up to lace through Luke's hair while her body pressed against his.

His quickened, shallow breathing sounded in her ears as sweetly as a symphony. His strong arms tightened around her when she tentatively caressed his tongue with the tip of hers.

Distantly she realized that he was easing her away from him. Her objection rose in her throat but she forced it back down, struggling with her disappointment, with her distress that she'd been so lost in his kiss that she'd forgotten her resolve.

Luke unerringly picked her house key from the others on the ring, and leaned past her to unlock and open her front door. The light she'd left on in the living room shone softly into the entrance hall.

He placed her keys in her palm and curled her fingers around them with his much larger hand. Then he lowered his face to hers and endowed her lips with a tender, lingering kiss.

"We'll see," he said.

Without another word, he strode down the walkway, slid behind the wheel of his car and drove into the night.

She watched until the red taillights disappeared, his softly spoken words echoing in her ears.

We'll see.

Chapter Six

Luke looked down the long, granite-surfaced meeting table at the faces of the men and women involved with making Blue Bonnet Park—an innovative industrial park—a reality. "All right," he said. "I think we've pretty well covered everything. Eugene, I want that status report on my desk tomorrow."

Eugene, who looked like a young linebacker for the Houston Oilers, nodded. "Consider it done."

Josh remained after the others had left. He finished placing papers in his black, ostrich-hide briefcase, then snapped it closed.

"Want to go grab some lunch?" Luke asked.

Josh stood. "Yeah," he said absently. A small furrow appeared between his eyebrows. "There may be trouble brewing, big brother."

"Trouble?"

"A reliable source warned me that you have an enemy in Newton Lockington."

Luke's jaw tightened. He and the county commissioner had butted horns several times. "Anyone not willing to fork over a bribe to Lockington is his enemy. The man is corrupt."

"You won't find any argument with that here. He gives politicians a bad name, and that's sayin' something. But it's because he's scum that you need to watch your back. Just be careful, okay?"

"I will. Now how about that lunch? I've got a meeting across town at one, so I can't take long."

They talked about Blue Bonnet as they rode the elevator down and walked out onto the street, heading to their favorite lunchtime restaurant.

"Why aren't you having lunch with the fair Gloria?" Josh asked after giving the waitress his order, then handing her his menu.

"She doesn't take lunch breaks."

Josh grinned. "Not even with a good-lookin' stud like you?"

Luke leaned back in his wrought-iron chair and released a frustrated sigh. "Not with me, good, bad or ugly. She's avoiding me, Josh."

Josh's grin faded. "Are you serious? Jeez, that's rough. I haven't seen you like this over a woman since…well, since Barbara. So, why do you think Gloria's avoiding you?"

"She believes we're incompatible. Not suited, is the way she puts it."

"And what do you think?"

Luke crushed his cloth napkin in his fist. When he spoke, his voice was level. "I think there's something about me that's got her worried. I only wish I knew what it was. Whatever it is, she seems to forget about it when we're together."

"Maybe that's what's really got her worried. You know—" Josh gave Luke a knowing look "—sexual attraction blinding common sense."

"I thought of that, but I can't see why her common sense would be warning her away from me."

"Maybe it's not you," Josh said quietly. "Maybe it's your family. Based on the little I know about the lady, she's conservative, traditional. Look what she does for a living. She

might be nervous over getting involved with one of the wild
Cahills.''

"Maybe at first, but I really think she's gotten past that."

"You mean your notorious family has already been dis-
cussed?"

The waitress came with their orders and, after refilling
their tea glasses, left without a word. Luke eyed his Reuben
sandwich.

"She reads the papers, Josh. And the guy in the sandwich shop downstairs has apparently supplied her with still
more lurid details of Cahill public exploits."

Josh flipped his hand as he finished chewing a bite of
coleslaw. "He's just sore because you don't buy *his* sandwiches."

"It's not like there aren't a million dirty little details he
could tell her about the Cahills." But somehow, Luke didn't
think that was it. There was something else, something more
specific, more personal, but he couldn't decipher from her
behavior what might be causing her reserve. "Oh, well.
Talking about it with anyone but her won't solve anything." He diverted the conversation to Poppy, then on to
business.

But Luke found he couldn't keep his mind on business.
Gloria hadn't kissed him with any reservation last Saturday
night, he thought with satisfaction. And their date was still
on for tomorrow night. Real Lady Test Number Two would
take place as scheduled, and he'd see what kind of taste she
had in homemaking. When he'd gone to pick her up for the
barbecue, he'd failed to notice anything but her and her
bird.

Tomorrow he'd do better. He'd stay focused on the test at
hand, and during the course of the evening, maybe he'd
uncover just why she thought they were so unsuited.

Gloria heard the doorbell from the kitchen, where she was
slicing the last of the loquats to be arranged on the saddle of
venison when it came out of the oven. She looked up at the
clock on the wall. Well, Luke might be unorthodox, but he
was certainly prompt.

Quickly she wiped her hands on a tea towel, then hurried toward the front door, pausing only to check herself in the reproduction George III gilt-wood mirror that hung in the entry hall. She reminded herself that the only reason she'd invited Luke to dinner was to allow him to see, without the distractions of his family, just how little he and she had in common. She felt the need to remind herself of that again as she turned the doorknob and came face-to-face with him.

"Good evening, Ms. Hamilton," Luke said cheerfully. He held a bouquet of wildflowers in one hand and a bottle of wine in the other. His gaze lingered on her face before continuing on to take in her mabe pearl earrings, her plum-colored shantung sheath and the wide sterling-silver cuff on her right wrist. Then slowly his gaze slid down her legs, with their black stockings, to her black patent pumps. "You're looking especially lovely tonight."

"And you're looking quite debonair, Mr. Cahill." In fact, she didn't want to take her eyes off him.

His hair glowed like molten gold, a vivid contrast to his dark, tailor-made suit. Tonight he was all elegance and power, like some Renaissance prince. Tall and broad shouldered and lean, he carried himself with a masculine grace that licked at her, sizzled through her, leaving her hungry for more than mere food. Much more.

Startled by the force of her desire, she tried to push it down. Self-consciously she smiled.

He leaned down and stole a hot, sweet kiss that left her blinking and slightly disoriented. His woodsy scent stroked across her swirling senses.

"Would you like to put these in water?" he asked, handing her the bouquet.

"Oh. Yes, yes, of course." She took the flowers from him and walked into the kitchen. He followed her. Leaning his shoulder against the doorframe, he watched her arrange them in a cut-glass vase.

Wasn't that just like Luke to bring wildflowers instead of the more predictable roses, she thought, as her fingers moved unerringly to create a picture-perfect composition, taking pleasure in the various colors and shapes.

"Would you like a drink?" she asked. "We have about twenty minutes before the venison will be done."

He requested a bourbon and branch water, which she poured into a crystal tumbler. As she handed it to him, the ice cubes tinkled softly against the side of the glass. She poured herself a chilled white wine, then led the way into her living room, where she set the flowers on a rosewood sofa table. Mozart wafted softly from the small speakers of the CD player concealed in the Irish wardrobe.

"Where's Hamlet tonight?" Luke asked as he looked around the room, seeming to approve.

"Upstairs. I put him to bed early. Otherwise you might not have had a moment's peace. He really is taken with you."

Luke gave her a lazy smile. "I'm told I have a way with animals and children."

And women, Gloria thought. He definitely had a way with women. At least, this woman.

He asked her about the unusual pieces displayed in her tall curio cabinet, and she related the country of origin and the story behind each treasure.

He took a sip of his drink consideringly. "The masks, the sword, the carvings—they're all from developing countries. Most of them have had civil wars in their recent history."

"That's right. My father didn't exactly pull the plum assignments."

"You lived in all these places." It was a statement, not a question.

"Yes, I have."

"Life must have been very...unpredictable," he observed.

"Yes." Unpredictable, unstable, and dangerous.

The timer went off, and Gloria gratefully escaped back to the kitchen. Swiftly she sliced the venison, laid it out on a silver-rimmed china serving platter, then added the garnish. She set it in the microwave oven to stay warm as she removed optical-glass plates of endive salad from the refrigerator and placed them on the dining table, which she'd earlier set with the china and silver she'd inherited from her mother. The crystal stemware she'd put out was a fabulous flea-market find she'd practically stolen from the vendor, and the malachite bowl that she'd filled with wisteria to serve as the centerpiece had come from an estate sale, as had the white damask tablecloth and napkins.

Luke opened the bottle of wine and nudged it down into the ice bucket. Then Gloria carried in the fragrant, freshly baked rolls from the kitchen, and he bore the platter of garnished venison.

"Where are the candles?" he asked.

Gloria had not wanted to lower the lighting, hoping to keep the dinner as neutral as possible. She was supposed to be demonstrating how unsuitable they were for each other, *not* setting the mood for romance.

Then why did you go to such trouble to prepare him a gourmet meal? asked that annoying little voice that seemed to live under her conscience. *Why did you take such pains to look nice for him?*

Without a word, she retrieved two ivory-colored beeswax candles and inserted them in crystal candlesticks. Luke promptly produced a book of matches and lit the wicks. Then he flipped off the wall switch and adjusted the illumination in the living room and kitchen until the light in the dining area was low and golden.

He moved around behind her and drew out her chair. Excruciatingly aware of his nearness, she allowed him to seat her and restrained herself from watching him as he moved to his own place across the small table. Oh, why hadn't she left that table leaf in? It would have provided a safer distance from him, from his magnetic potency.

She relaxed a bit as Luke proved himself to be a perfect guest. He was entertaining and witty. He amused her with tales from his childhood, when he and Josh had spent a great deal of time getting into mischief. He complimented her outrageously over the food and her home, and she found herself glowing with pleasure.

Luke helped her clear away the dirty dishes and leaned his hips against the countertop as she made the coffee that

would accompany their tangerine soufflé dessert. "You said
your mother died when you were twelve," he mused.
"Where did you learn to be such a great cook? And your
home—it should be on the cover of a magazine. You're a
great hostess."

Gloria stiffened as she pulled the dessert plates from the
cabinet. Yes, she was a good hostess. Charles had admired
that about her, too. And in the end, she'd discovered, that's
all he'd ever really wanted her for. With an effort, she suppressed her reaction to Luke's words.

"Who taught you these things?" he asked.

"Alice took over the duties of raising me. My father had
little time. Anyway, Alice insisted that I learn to cook like a
chef, to entertain. She taught me to be an excellent hostess." Gloria's cold lips sketched a smile. "She thought it
would increase the chances of my having a happy marriage."

"I guess Alice hadn't bargained on creeps like Charles
Elliot."

A stone dropped into the pit of her stomach. He knew.

While her divorce had never been a secret, it certainly
hadn't made the newspapers as Josh and his wife's had.
Gloria had always been certain that the matter was of no
interest to anyone other than her, Charles and, of course, his
new wife, and Gloria had taken comfort in that knowledge.
Now that small security had been stripped away.

She stared down at the uneaten soufflé on her plate. If
Luke knew about her divorce, then he probably also knew
that she'd been less important to her husband than his sexy
secretary. Unbidden, the image of Charles, his trousers
down around his ankles, his buttocks bare as he bucked between Suzette's spread thighs flashed into her mind with
hideous clarity.

Luke's voice called her back from that traumatic moment.

"You're a woman of many talents, Gloria Hamilton," he
said softly. His eyes were blue fire, and she felt their heat lap
against her skin, leaving her feeling flushed and tingling.
"All this and you have your own business, too."

She looked up at him. Business? She'd never met a man who was impressed because she had her own business. Unless they needed the service she offered, they wrote Hamilton Consulting off as fluff. So you teach manners, they'd say, when they said anything at all. Lately, of course, she hadn't really talked with that many men socially. Most of the males she dealt with, aside from the dry cleaner, the vice president at her bank, Fred and his catering assistant and the guy in the sandwich shop, were her clients, and she never dated clients.

"You're very kind," she murmured.

"Kindness has nothing to do with it," Luke said. "It's the truth." He reached across the table and took her hand in his. "You've weathered a divorce—"

Heat throbbed in her face. "You know."

"Tidewater's a small town, Gloria, with not much going on. So everyone keeps an eye on Houston. And in Houston, Charles Elliot moved in high circles."

She remembered a time when Charles had been a world away from those circles. His poor-boy manners and speech had barred him from the society he'd been so desperate to join.

She forced her lips into a polite smile. "More coffee?"

He ignored her offer. "Look, I know it's none of my business—"

"It's not."

"But Charles Elliot is a fool."

"A very successful one." Success she'd helped him attain. All the time, she'd thought they'd been building a future together. Oh, there'd been a fool in that marriage, all right.

He raised her hand to his lips, never taking his gaze from hers. "He's unworthy of our discussion." His breath puffed against the back of her hand, just before his lips brushed lightly over that warm spot, sending a tingling trail through her arm, into her body, where it spread into a glow.

Her mind tumbled with the sensations his mere touch sparked in her.

"I'll help you with the dishes," he said.

She cleared her throat, trying to regain her aplomb. "That won't be necessary."

He smiled. "I insist. It's the least I can do after the trouble you took to make this wonderful dinner."

She started to insist that she could clear away later, but stopped herself. Here the man was offering to help her clean up these dirty dishes. Why shouldn't she enjoy his assistance?

Gloria smiled back at him. "Okay."

They each donned white chef's aprons, and between the two of them, they returned the dining table and the kitchen to their usual tidy order, teasing and laughing as they worked.

"It's time I left," he said, taking off his apron.

Surprised, Gloria glanced at the kitchen clock. Good grief! Where had the time gone?

He slipped on his jacket, then turned to her. "Thank you for a wonderful dinner. I had a great time. Must be the company."

"Must be." She wished the evening could go on and on. This man was irresistible, irrepressible and downright sexy. He made *her* feel sexy.

Luke moved close to her, but he didn't touch her. "Maybe we're not so ill suited, after all."

She thought of how quickly the evening had sped away. Luke's glances, his words, made her feel like a desirable woman. She'd discovered that she wanted to hear more stories about his boyhood. She wanted to learn all about him. Maybe it was because a devilish light gleamed in his eyes when he smiled at her. Or maybe it was the way his deep laughter sent a thrill through her and brought an answering smile to her lips. Or maybe... maybe it was because something in her responded to him, to the sight and sound and scent of him. Certainly Charles had never made her feel this way. What element about Luke Cahill called to her, excited her? She wanted to find out.

Maybe we're not so ill suited, after all.

She wasn't willing to go that far, she decided, but she wanted to learn more about Luke, about the way he made her feel—alive.

"Maybe not," she equivocated.

When he looked at her, she went willingly into his arms, eager for the heady experience of his kiss. Her fingers found their way up his shoulders to thread through the heavy mass of his hair. His arms tightened slightly around her body. His tongue rubbed sensuously against hers. The rhythm of his breath hastened.

A fierce yearning cut through Gloria. She needed to be looked at as a woman. Not a hostess. Not a means to an end. A woman. *Can't a man want me for myself, not for the help I'll be to his career or social standing?*

Luke's hands rubbed restlessly up and down her back, the solidity of his chest pressed against her. The earth spun in a giddy whirl as his mouth moved over hers.

Luke straightened and firmly set her away from him at arm's length. His color ran high, and his hair stood on end where her fingers had laced through. He sucked in a deep breath, held it a second, then huffed it out.

"I think I'd better leave now," he said.

She reached up to smooth his hair, and he caught her hand in his.

"I think it might be a good idea to keep your distance, lady. You have an effect on me like no woman I've ever met before."

Gloria brightened, feeling ridiculously delighted with that news. It was as if her prayers had been answered. "Really?"

He nodded slowly, without taking his eyes from hers or releasing her hand. "Uh-huh."

Emboldened, she took a step closer to him. "What kind of effect?"

"That's close enough. I think you know what I'm talking about. And I've always been taught not to play with fire."

Gloria gave him what she hoped was a smile that was as seductive as she was feeling. "Playing?" she asked, dropping her voice to a husky purr. "Is that what we were doing?"

The pulse in the side of his neck quickened. "Oh, yeah. We were playing, all right. But—" He broke off as she threaded her fingers through his.

For brief seconds, she witnessed what must have been an inner struggle, judging from the ferocious expression on his face.

"Aw, hell," he swore and pulled her back into his arms. "Just...one...more...kiss," he muttered distractedly between kisses.

"Just...one," she agreed.

Five minutes later, Luke tore his mouth away from hers, his hair mussed, his tie askew. She noticed a small smudge of her lipstick on his cheek. "That's it." He panted, releasing her. "I'm going now."

Too breathless to speak, Gloria just nodded.

"Okay." He opened the front door and stepped backward out onto her front porch. "I'm gone." He closed the door.

Gloria stood where she was, incapable of doing more at that moment. She heard a knock, then the door opened again to reveal Luke.

"Next Saturday?" he said. "The movies?"

"All—all right."

"Good. Lock your door." He shut it with a firm thump.

Josh lowered the blueprints he was studying. "You're whistling again."

Luke scanned the noisy construction site of Gulf Breeze. In five months there would be a mall here, adjoined by a large hotel and a high-rise office building. "Am I?"

"Yes. You've been whistling all week, and it's beginning to get on my nerves. No man should be so happy. It's unnatural."

"I'm going to see her tomorrow evening." Anticipation revved inside Luke at the prospect.

Josh sighed. "Why don't you just marry the woman and be done with it? Then you can be as miserable as the rest of us."

Luke grinned, unable to stop himself. Thoughts of Gloria did that to him. She was shaping up to be his dream woman. She got along with his family. She liked children. She had elegant taste and could cook. Her beauty was a nice plus, too, but if he was being honest with himself, he knew what he felt for Gloria went beyond mere appreciation of her refined taste and culinary skills. True, she set his blood simmering as no woman had before. Her sweet response in his arms heated him with primitive satisfaction. Still, it was more; it went deeper.

About this polished, self-sufficient woman there was a concealed vulnerability. In rare moments, he caught glimpses of it, only to find her strength back in place in the next instant. A haunted look. A quivering at the corners of her mouth. A shimmering in averted eyes. It pierced him with an unexpected tenderness. If ever there was a woman who needed cherishing, she was Gloria Hamilton. And the more time Luke spent with her, the more he wanted to be the man to render that cherishing.

"I *said,* why don't you just marry her and be done with it?" Josh repeated, raising his voice slightly, as if to penetrate Luke's preoccupation.

"I heard you," Luke said. "But unlike about twenty men in my family, I'm not looking for a weekend courtship. I don't want to have to do it again with another woman in two years because the first marriage failed. When I walk down that aisle, the woman on my arm will be my dream bride, not someone I just met."

Josh lifted a blond eyebrow. "Is that so? Well, as I recall, you were talking about marriage right after you met Gloria."

"I can talk all I want, but it doesn't become permanent until the wedding. The operative word here is *permanent.* I'm getting to know Gloria now."

"Oh? And just what have you learned, O Wise One?"

"I've learned she likes children. She seemed to get along with everyone she met at the barbecue, and she really hit it off with Poppy and Maudie. Even that wife of Zack's— what's her name? The charmer with the dyed black hair?"

"Tiffany."

"Tiffany. Of course. Gloria even got along with her and her kids."

"Just what's wrong with Tiffany?"

"She's inappropriate for Zack. She's embarrassed him countless times at corporate functions with that New York company of his."

"Zack told you this?"

"Cousin Peggy works there, too."

"Cousin Peggy is a gossipy little witch."

Luke had to concede that was true. Peggy did thrive on carrying tales. But he'd witnessed for himself Tiffany's— and about twenty-four other Cahill wives'—tasteless makeup and attire, their loud, twanging voices spewing lousy grammar, and their poor manners.

He'd had a crude, loud, brassy mother. That was enough. His wife would be nothing like that.

Josh shot Luke a skeptical look. "Are you sure you're really looking at Gloria? I mean, are you seeing the woman or her refinement?"

"Both," Luke said firmly.

"Have you slept with her yet?"

Luke scowled at his brother. "What the hell kind of question is that?"

"A practical one," Josh said, unfazed. "Sex does figure into marriage, you know. What if all her social graces are nothing but a cover-up for frigidity? Bimbo wives might run in our family, but as you might have noticed, they're usually hot little numbers. A man needs to find these things out before he slips that ring on a woman's finger."

Luke remembered how ardently Gloria responded to his kisses. "A short skirt and a low-cut blouse don't guarantee that a woman's a sexual firecracker, Josh."

"All I'm saying, big brother, is that you need to look to see that Gloria, not her social skills, is what you want."

"Thank you, Dr. Cahill," Luke said dryly. "I think I'll be able to remember that."

"Next time make an appointment with my secretary. These out-of-office consultations are breaking me."

"If you've finished handing out advice, maybe you won't mind if we get back to work."

Josh grinned. "Yeah, you need the money. You'll soon be paying for a wedding."

"So when am I going to meet your gentleman friend?" Alice asked as she laid a pile of letters to be signed on the desk in front of Gloria.

"You see him almost every day in the lobby. You said so yourself." Gloria quickly scratched her name on the first letter and set it aside.

Alice folded her arms over her formidable bosom. "Now listen, dearie," she said in a no-nonsense tone of voice. "I'm as close to a mum as you have. I've a *duty* to meet your young man."

Guiltily, Gloria worried her bottom lip between her teeth. Alice had been a mother and friend for most of her life, and she was indeed entitled to meet a man about whom Gloria might be serious. Alice hadn't been in Texas to meet Charles, and look what had happened with that relationship. But Gloria couldn't claim a serious relationship with Luke. "I'm just dating him, Alice. It's not significant."

"Those aren't the signs I'm seeing."

Gloria shifted in her executive chair. "It's only that I haven't really dated for a while. And you've got to admit, Luke Cahill is something special."

Alice fixed Gloria with a stern eye. "As well he should be. *You* are something special, and any man who's not blind, deaf and dumb is bound to realize that." She shook her finger at Gloria. "And don't you even mention that wretch, Charles Elliot. His brains are all below his belt. You're well-off without the likes of him, my girl. Good riddance to bad rubbish, I say. That tart he took up with is no better than he deserves."

A smile tugged at Gloria's lips. "I wouldn't dare suggest that I'm not the catch of the year, Alice. I'd have you to answer to."

Alice tried to maintain her severe expression, but the twitching at the corners of her mouth gave her away. After a minute, she gave up and chuckled. "I'll not have you selling yourself short. Your new fellow may be something special, but that's only as it should be. And that doesn't alter the fact that I haven't met him."

"Yes, Miss Brackenbury," Gloria said, feigning the manner of a properly chastened schoolgirl even as she made a mental note to arrange the introduction. She'd move heaven and earth to keep from hurting her friend's feelings. Alice had done too much, given up too much for Gloria, to ever be overlooked.

"You've met Vern," Alice added pointedly.

"So I have. Small world, his working for Texas Gulf Properties."

"Not so small. Half of Tidewater works for TGP."

"Well, maybe not half. A quarter. An eighth."

"A lot."

"Yes, a lot. Operating heavy machinery for one of the largest employers in town must be a pretty stable job, don't you think?"

Alice regarded Gloria with narrowed eyes. "Yes."

"When is the man going to marry you? I mean, he's been courting you for months. Is he serious or what? I won't have him toying with your affections, Alice. If he thinks he can trifle with you, well, I'll soon show him the error of his ways."

A tickled smile took over Alice's face. "I'll convey your message."

"Or bring him to me, and I'll convey it myself."

Holding up her hands as if to ward off Gloria's offer, Alice backed out of the room. "No. No, that's quite all right. I'd much rather speak to him myself. He's so tenderhearted, you understand. Wouldn't want to wound the man, now, would we?" She hastened away toward her own desk in the reception area.

Gloria leaned back in her reupholstered executive chair, pleased with her small victory. Dollars to doughnuts Vern popped the question to Alice before Gloria even found a man with whom she might consider marriage.

Oh, she wanted to marry again, of course. She wanted a family, and heaven only knew how fast her biological clock was ticking. But mostly she wanted a man she could trust. A man who would look at her and see *her,* not some Miss Manners or Hostess of the Year.

Luke made her feel as if she was the most exciting, desirable woman in Texas. Quite a feat, she thought, considering how dull she really was. She had to face the fact than an exciting man like him would soon tire of her.

Dull, but dependable. Still, in a world where loyalties and policies changed daily, dependable was getting harder and harder to find. Surely there was a nice, predictable man out there who would be content with a nice, dependable woman?

Meanwhile, for a short time at least, she had Luke. She'd enjoy their time together while it lasted, before he concluded that she wasn't going to spring from her conservative, commonsense cocoon as an exotic butterfly, ready to live on the whim of the breeze. No, she'd be the brown moth clutching a flight plan and a meteorological chart. She was done with unpredictability.

But she'd savor Luke's company as long as she could. At least she'd have memories....

Tomorrow night would be part of those memories. He was taking her to a movie, but so far he'd evaded telling her which one. Odd. But there was that whimsy factor again. He was probably waiting until the last moment to see what he "felt like."

That was the way with butterfly types.

The whir of the old-fashioned film projector was barely audible over Melanie's deathbed words to Scarlett about Rhett, and Gloria's occasional hiccuped sob. Luke gently tugged the wadded, saturated hankie from Gloria's fingers. She never took her teary eyes from the ancient screen that

stood eight feet in front of their lawn chairs in her backyard.

He smiled to himself as he handed her a fresh handkerchief. Who would have suspected that professional, polished Gloria wept at sad movies? This unexpected senti-
mentality pleased him, though he couldn't say why. Maybe
he just enjoyed seeing her softer side.

"To be or not to be," Hamlet muttered in Luke's ear. The
bird adjusted his footing, and Luke felt the small shift in
weight on his shoulder.

It would have been a whole lot easier just to rent a TV, a
VCR and a video of *Gone With the Wind,* but Luke had
thought it lacked ambience. So he'd tracked down old reels
of the movie, persuaded a friend to lend him the projector,
then rescued this home movie screen from the attic at White
Oaks. He'd loaded up two lawn chairs in his truck with the
rest of the carefully secured and tarped equipment. On his
way to Gloria's, he'd stopped and bought candy, sodas and
a couple of buckets of popcorn from a movie theater, then
come a-courtin'.

"I'll think about that tomorrow," Gloria murmured,
dabbing at her eyes with the handkerchief Luke had
thoughtfully provided. Sitting here with him under the stars,
the images of fifty-odd years ago playing across the silvery
old screen, the salty smell of buttered popcorn and the lan-
guid perfume from the honeysuckle on her backyard fence
mingling with the clean scent of newly cut wood for the siding the workmen had left stacked next to the house, she
thought this had to be one of the most romantic evenings
she'd ever experienced. Never in a million years had she expected this outdoor "theater" when he'd suggested the
movies.

"Welcome," Hamlet squawked from his perch on Luke's
broad shoulder. "Welcome."

"So... did you like the film?" Luke asked. He touched
her hair with his fingertips.

She smiled up at him. His beautiful, masculine face was
night shadowed, the moon painting his forehead, the bridge
of his nose, one cheekbone and his full bottom lip with

molten silver. "Oh, yes," she said, wishing her voice didn't sound so breathless. "This was such a wonderful idea." His powerfully sensual presence stroked over her like a tingling tongue. His carefully arranged surprise for her had been evidence of Luke's serendipity, and Gloria knew she should be congratulating herself on being proved correct. The newspapers and the guy in the sandwich shop had been right. Luke Cahill was indeed unpredictable.

But she wouldn't worry about that now. He made her feel wonderful, and, she told herself, there was no harm in enjoying that while it lasted. She was safe enough. After all, it wasn't as if she was going to marry the guy or anything. As he leaned closer, his breath stirring tendrils of her hair, she shivered with desire.

It was the "or anything" that she worried might prove lethal.

Chapter Seven

Luke stared at the telephone on his desk. It was time to get Real Lady Test Number Three under way. What kind of hostess for business occasions was Gloria? That's what test three was all about. It was important, he told himself stubbornly. As his wife, she would be expected to oversee certain social functions. Too many times he'd seen his cousins, his own *brother,* embarrassed.

Of course, Gloria wasn't like any of them. He glared at the telephone. Aw, hell. He really hated this.

A double knock sounded at his office door, but before he could growl an answer, Josh entered, beaming. A large, colorful sheet of paper fluttered from the careful grip of his fingers.

"Howdy, big brother," Josh said. He grinned proudly. "Look what Poppy painted."

At the mention of Poppy's name, Luke brightened. "A new masterpiece from my favorite niece?"

Josh held up a watercolor of the Victorian Italianate mansion that now housed the Tidewater Historical Society. "Not bad, huh? You can tell it's Mumford House just by looking at it."

Little Poppy definitely had a gift, Luke thought, but in all honesty, he had to admit that the real reason it was easy to tell this painting was of Mumford House instead of any of the myriad other big white Victorian houses in Tidewater was the distinctive fountain in the front. Water flowed from the crossed pink marble barrels of two eleven-feet-high Colt navy model pistols.

"She's talented, that's for sure," Luke said. "Maybe we should hire an art teacher."

"There's plenty of time for that. Let the kid just have fun with it for now." Josh carefully rolled the painting into a tube. "Poppy asked me to give this to Gloria."

Luke took his niece's preference for Gloria as a good omen. It was the first time Poppy had indicated a liking for an adult outside the family or the White Oaks staff.

"Maudie called. Bunnie actually came over to see Poppy this morning."

"It's about damn time."

"Yeah. Maudie said Bunnie and about twenty-five of our cousins-in-law have set up a special ongoing class with Gloria. They don't want their husbands to know about it, so they've been meeting at her house."

"Why don't they want their husbands to know?" Luke asked.

Josh shrugged. "Pride, I guess."

So the bimbo brides were quietly trying to acquire some social polish. Luke felt a twinge of guilt. He knew he hadn't made Bunnie's life easy while she'd been married to Josh. She'd been a continual screwup and embarrassment, and on several occasions it had taken everything Luke had to remain silent.

"Well, if anyone can help them, Gloria can," he said, trying to temper with reality the surge of hope that rose in him. Best not to expect miracles.

"It's not like they have a deadly disease, Luke," Josh said softly.

"Mom started out as a bimbo." She'd vengefully dragged all their lives into a hell of humiliation.

Josh gazed out the window at the Gulf beyond. "Yeah."

"Bunnie's record as a mother hasn't exactly been exemplary."

"I know."

Luke wanted better for his children. He wanted better for himself, as well. He wanted a woman who could hold her own with him, one he could respect. He wouldn't settle for less than a woman who wanted the same things he did: companionship, children, a strong family life. He believed Gloria was that woman, but he had to make sure. *He had to.* He couldn't live like his father had, all knotted up inside with jealousy, anger and grief until only the oblivion of liquor could offer relief. Luke would not allow his own sons or daughters to suffer what he and Josh had gone through—the futile hope, the shame, the tearing neglect.

Too much was at stake. As much as Luke wanted to forgo this next test and concentrate on courting her, he couldn't take the risk. He was crazy about Gloria, and that worried him. How trustworthy was his own judgment where women were concerned when just about every other man in his family had made the wrong choice? Believing he was different from them might be pure, disastrous arrogance. He couldn't afford to chance it. He'd been wrong before. Humiliatingly, painfully wrong.

"Well, I'd better get this picture down to Gloria," Josh said. "I've got a meeting with a possible tenant for Blue Bonnet."

After Josh had gone, Luke leaned back in his chair and doggedly formulated the words he'd use to involve Gloria in Real Lady Test Number Three.

"I have a favor to ask," Luke's voice said over the phone line.

Gloria smiled as she cradled the telephone handset between her ear and shoulder. Her fountain pen scratched lightly against the paper as she signed the typed letters Alice had stacked on her desk. "Ask away," she said, rolling her shoulder to adjust the receiver to a more comfortable position.

"Week after next I'm going to be taking an important new prospect and his wife to my family's hunting lodge in the Hill Country. They're Swedish, and I'm not familiar with their customs. I..." His voice died away. He cleared his throat and continued. "Would you consider being my hostess? I need someone who knows something about Swedish ways, someone who can oversee the caterer. I'd like that someone to be you."

A freezing chill flowed through Gloria. She straightened slowly in her chair. Her fingers curled tightly around the handset.

"Gloria?"

Her stomach churned. She'd been used as a hostess before. *Used.* She was good at what she did, damned good, but her work wasn't *who* she was. Didn't anyone care about that? Didn't any man want *her?*

"Gloria? Are you there?"

"Yes." The word came out a choking rasp from a dry, tight throat. "Yes, I'm here."

"Is everything all right?" She heard the worry in his voice.

No! I thought you were interested in me for me, *not for my social skills.* The nightmare, the anguish, flooded back, biting deeply into her heart. *I thought you liked me!*

She drew in a deep, unsteady breath. "Everything is...fine. Just fine."

"Did you hear me?"

"I heard."

"I'd expect to compensate you, of course," he blurted.

She frowned. Gradually her frown eased into puzzlement. Good Lord. He was nervous!

He cleared his throat again. "I said, I'd expect—"

"I heard what you said."

Silence filled the telephone line.

Finally he spoke. "Is there a problem?"

"I'll have to think about it."

"You don't know if there's a problem?"

"Normally, Mr. Cahill," she said in her best business voice, "I don't hire out for parties."

"This isn't a party, honest. Just a quiet weekend with some nice Swedish folks. Do you ride? You can get in some horseback riding. Nice scenery. You'll really like the scenery—"

"Actually, Mr. Cahill, I don't hire out at all."

"I didn't mean to insult you. It's just that I need your help, and I want you with me. I'd like you to help guide me through the mine fields of social—"

"I'm afraid I have to go now. Alice is signaling me that my next appointment is here." Alice was nowhere in sight. Judging from the clacking of the keyboard, she was working at her computer in the reception area.

"Gloria, what's wrong? You're upset with me, I can tell. What did I do?"

"I really must go."

"Damn it, Gloria." Frustration rumbled through his voice. "Just tell me what I did wrong. I asked you because you're an expert on such things, and I'm not. I thought it would be more comfortable for the Adkissons, especially Mrs. Adkisson, if there was another woman there. I mean, if I was a couple. No, that's not exactly right. I mean—"

"That's okay. I think I get the picture. I've got to go now—"

"Gloria—"

"Goodbye." She quickly hung up, unwilling to talk more on the subject. Her hands trembled slightly as she curled them around the armrests on her chair. She didn't want to think about Luke's request, about the heartsick memories it stirred up. Right now, she didn't want to think about anything. If she could just shake off all those terrible feelings of not quite measuring up, of not being woman enough to really interest a man.

She checked her calendar and saw the two remaining hours of the workday were clear of appointments. Grabbing her purse, she bolted from the office, offering a keen-eyed Alice the excuse of not feeling well. It was true. She didn't feel at all well. Confused, shaky, on the verge of tears—not well.

When she got home, she took the telephone off the hook and pulled all the curtains closed. As if sensing his human's unhappiness, Hamlet insisted upon taking his place on her shoulder. He nuzzled her cheek, soothing her with the satin feel of his feathers. She found his small mutters comforting.

Despite the fact that it was warm, and her air conditioner was humming away, Gloria made herself some hot chocolate and topped it with whipped cream and a single bright maraschino cherry. Then she scooped up some of Hamlet's favorite seed and fruit mix and retreated to the deepest, most comfortable chair in the living room, where she sipped her steaming drink and fed her feathered companion bits of his treat.

Gradually, Gloria recaptured her calm. The quaking in her middle eased away, and the sharpness of that hollow, desolate feeling faded. History wasn't repeating itself, she told herself over and over. Luke wasn't anything like Charles. He already possessed everything that her ex-husband had used her to gain: social standing, power, wealth. To Charles, she'd been a mere tool—the diplomat's daughter. To Luke she was...what? Why was he even interested in her? Aside, of course, from his admiration of her derriere.

She set her empty cup on the chair-side table, then reached up to stroke Hamlet. He made small, contented noises in his throat. Well, why shouldn't Luke be interested in her? she told herself stoutly.

Because you're dull, a small, insidious voice answered from deep within her. *Isn't that why your husband looked elsewhere? Isn't that why your father found so little time for you? Dull.*

True.

Gloria straightened abruptly, and Hamlet squawked a protest as he flapped his wings to keep his balance. All right, she might be dull, but maybe Luke Cahill *liked* dull women. Maybe he didn't care at all if she was dull. Maybe, just maybe, he could teach her how to liven up a little.

She sighed. All the man had done was to ask if she'd act as hostess to a business prospect and his wife for a weekend. Wasn't it only natural for Luke to turn to her? These clients were important to him, and he knew she possessed the expertise to smooth the path to whatever business arrangement he sought. Luke had expected to pay her, which surely meant he saw his request of her as mere business, separate from his personal relationship. After all, Luke Cahill could afford to hire someone from the UN and fly them in for the weekend, if he wanted to. Maybe she should feel flattered that he'd turned to her. Well, maybe flattered was stretching it.

Gloria walked into the kitchen and put her cup into the dishwasher. She glanced at the refrigerator. She knew she ought to eat dinner, but she wasn't hungry. She felt emotionally drained and physically fatigued. Although it was only nine o'clock, she decided to call it an evening and go to bed.

She put Hamlet in his cage for the night and, murmuring a good-night, dropped the cover into place. As she trudged down the second-story hall to her bedroom, she reflected that she must learn to be less touchy. It wasn't healthy to allow the past to eat into her present like corroding acid. Everything it touched would become poisoned, until all she'd have left would be her worst memories.

Luke wasn't Charles, she thought wearily as she burrowed beneath the covers. He wouldn't deceive her. Tomorrow she'd call and agree to help him with his Swedish guests.

Luke pulled his pickup truck into Gloria's driveway shortly after ten o'clock. He turned off the lights and the engine, but made no other move as he gazed at the darkened house. Was she even home?

He'd been trying to reach her on the telephone ever since he'd called her back after that crazy conversation this afternoon, and Alice had told him Gloria had gone home early. When he'd dialed her home number, he'd received a busy signal. Even a call to the telephone company had proved futile.

So he'd decided to give her time. Time to think over whatever was bothering her. But the more *he* thought it over, the worse that idea seemed. His plans for Real Lady Test Number Three were crumbling before his eyes. The hostess trial was important. All he had to do was remember Bunnie's copious weeping whenever she'd found herself in an awkward situation—which had happened all too frequently. Or Uncle Darnell's wife, Lottie, locking herself in the bedroom when nearly all the champagne bottles had exploded at her first—and only—fund-raiser luncheon. The guests and staff had been left milling around, wondering what was going on, until Maudie had arrived to take the situation in hand.

For more than the loss of his test, Luke found he needed to know Gloria was all right. What had caused her unexpected reaction? The thought of her being worried or upset thrust into his chest like a bowie knife. Worse, he couldn't shake the feeling that somehow he was responsible.

Maybe it was just the guilt over this testing business that was eating at him. After all, what had he said that could have prompted such a reaction from her? Yes, it must be the guilt, because he sure as hell didn't feel good about testing her. But guilt or not, he wanted to make certain that Gloria was well.

Quietly he got out of his truck, then went to her front door where he rang the bell and waited. And waited. And waited. Growing impatient with alarm, he rang again. Still no answer. He walked around to the garage and peered in the window. Through a chink in the blinds, he caught the reflection of moonlight on the light-colored paint job of her old sedan. Her car was home at least. That meant there was a greater chance she was, too. His stomach clenched. What if she was ill, so ill she couldn't get downstairs to open the door? Or even answer the phone?

That did it. Luke strode around to the back of her house, where the repair work on the old Victorian's siding had been taking place since last week. There, as he had expected, he found the twelve-foot ladder the workmen used. Luke decided to try Gloria's second-story windows first, thinking her bedroom would likely be up there.

The first window he squinted through seemed to be a study or office. He saw a desk, file cabinets, a long dark shape he thought must be a couch. But no bed. He tested the window. Locked.

Quickly, quietly, he descended the ladder and moved it over to the next window. Peering through a crack between the curtains, Luke thought he spied a shadowed form lying in the double bed.

She should have heard the doorbell, he fretted. It wasn't natural for anyone to sleep through it—not the way he'd leaned on the thing. She was ill. Ill and alone. Worried, he tapped on the window. Seconds later, no one had come, so he tapped again. Still no answer. Afraid for Gloria, determined to get inside to her, Luke tested the lock on the window. It had been set firmly in place. Luke swore under his breath. No option remained but to break the window.

Suddenly the window flew open.

"Just stay where you are and don't try anything funny!" Gloria shouted, waving a can of pepper spray in Luke's startled face.

Instinctively he lunged back, away from the weapon—almost away from the ladder. Feeling himself falling, he made a grab for the windowsill to steady himself.

Gloria must have thought he was trying to attack. With a strangled shriek, she sprayed the air with peppery fumes. Luke managed to snap his eyes shut before too much damage was done. Blindly, holding his breath, he launched himself through the noxious vapor into the clear air of the dark room. He landed at her feet with a bone-jarring thud on the oak floor.

She scrambled back and bolted out the door and down the hall. "I'm calling the police!"

Luke lay where he'd landed for minutes, gasping for breath, his eyes burning and watering, his nostrils feeling as if they were aflame. Finally he picked himself up, coughing. "Gloria . . . it's me . . . Luke. Don't be . . . afraid."

Fumbling around, he managed to find the bedside lamp and click it on. Then he raised his choked voice. "Did you . . . hear me? No one is trying to . . . hurt you." A paroxysm of coughing seized him.

Through the blur of tears, he saw her pale face, framed by a tumble of dark hair, peek cautiously around the doorframe. "Luke?"

He nodded. "Do you have . . . any . . . water?"

She hurried to him. "Oh, I'm so sorry! Come on. Let's go into the bathroom and see what I can do." She solicitously took his arm and guided him into the bathroom. Suddenly she straightened. "I'd better call the police back." She darted out the door.

Fifteen minutes later, he sat on the edge of the bathtub as she finished rinsing his eyes with bottled springwater. At least he didn't think he was going to die now.

"So," she said as she handed him a towel, "might one ask what you were doing on a ladder outside my window at this hour?"

He gave her a squint-eyed glare. "I was worried about you."

"I'm touched, of course, but wouldn't a simple phone call have sufficed?"

Annoyance rose from Luke's dented pride. "I tried. Your line was busy."

"Busy?" Her eyebrows drew down slightly in puzzlement. Then her face cleared. "Oh."

" 'Oh'? What's that supposed to mean?"

She lifted her chin at his tone. "I took my phone off the hook, but that still doesn't explain why you tried to break into my room."

"I told you. I was worried. I couldn't get through to you on the phone for hours. So I drove over here. I nearly pushed that damned doorbell through the wall, but you didn't answer."

"Oh."

"Another 'oh.' Don't tell me you disconnected the doorbell."

"No. It's just . . . well, you have to press it just right or it doesn't work."

Luke scowled. "How 'just right' can you press a door-bell? You put your finger on it and push."

"From an angle."

"Huh?"

A whisper of color tinged her cheeks. "You have to press the button from a certain angle and, you know, sort of . . . jiggle it."

"No, I don't know. I've never heard of having to jiggle a doorbell button."

"It's not working correctly, and I just haven't gotten around to getting it fixed. There. Is that plain enough for you? Now I have a question. What were you doing with a twelve-foot ladder? Is this a piece of equipment you always carry with you? On that *truck* I saw in the driveway when I got the springwater from the kitchen?"

This damned bathroom was about the size of a closet, Luke thought irritably, and it was closing in on him. He stalked out, back into her bedroom. When he turned around, he almost fell over her, not realizing she had stalked out after him. Now she stood facing him, her arms akimbo.

"Just what's wrong with my truck?" he demanded. "It's a good truck. I drive it all the time out on construction sites. It's never given me a moment's trouble." Which was more than he could say for any woman he'd ever known. "And that ladder belongs to the men working on your house. What did you think, anyway? That I was a cat burglar come to plunder your diamond tiara? Or a birdnapper ready to make off with Hamlet? Sure, I've only wheedled dates out of you because I wanted to scope out your house for my next heist." He rubbed his eyes.

She lightly batted his hands away from his face. "I've never seen you drive a truck."

"I've never seen you in a purple satin camisole and tap pants until tonight, but clearly that doesn't mean you don't own them." There was no denying how she owned them. They clung to her high, firm breasts and her curvaceous backside and left the long length of her legs completely naked.

She took a step back, silent on bare feet. Her gaze slid aside as she crossed her arms over her breasts like a shield. "I wasn't expecting company."

"I'm glad to hear that," he growled, feeling uncustomarily possessive. The thought of another man seeing her like this sent tension burning through him.

"*Not* that it's any of your business," she added stiffly.

He took the step that closed the distance between them and cupped her bare shoulders in his hands. In the low light of her bedside lamp, his eyes met hers. "I think we both know better than that."

Her gaze didn't waver. "Do we?"

In her softly spoken question, Luke heard nuances that plucked at him with hesitant, bittersweet fingers, and something inside him, something long hidden, responded. Hope bloomed like a seed receiving sunshine for the first time in years.

"I want to know," he said softly, "what I did to upset you."

"I— It wasn't you. It was my own problem." A ghost of a smile flitted over her lips. "I think I've worked it out."

"Tell me," he whispered against her ear. "Tell me so I'll know how not to hurt you."

Her eyes drifted closed and she shivered slightly against him. "You . . . you didn't hurt me. Really. You didn't."

"Good." Luke savored having her in his arms. The silk of her hair brushed against his jaw. Her skin was warm and smelled faintly of exotic flowers. An urge to protect her, to shield her from any harm in the world flared in him.

She placed her palm against his cheek. "You were really concerned, weren't you?" she asked, as if that fact amazed her.

"Yes." He set his hand over hers, enjoying the intimacy of both gestures. Turning his head, he pressed a lingering kiss into the cup of her palm. He felt her tense, then melt. He took advantage of the change to press closer to her. The fabric barrier of their clothes did little to mute the roundness of her breasts now firm against his chest. His body flamed in response.

A nighthawk's call drifted through the open window. An errant puff of breeze stirred the lace curtains.

Slowly he lowered his head, giving her a choice, giving her time to break free. She lifted her face to him, her lips parted in anticipation, causing his already heated blood to pound. Yearning and desire collided, howling through him with the force of a full-blown hurricane.

He claimed her mouth in an open, demanding kiss that seared away all trace of civility. His tongue rubbed shamelessly against hers in rampant carnality. Restlessly, his hands moved up and down her back. He charged ahead beyond reason, beyond anything but the need to claim Gloria's sweet, womanly body. She was his. *His.* Never again would a man hurt her or humiliate her. The beat of his blood through his veins drowned out reason. Hungrily he filled his hands with her luscious buttocks, kneading them through the glossy satin, holding her in place as he rubbed against her.

She caught her breath in a strangled, feral sound, piercing the back of his neck with her fingernails as she pressed closer to him. He pushed the spaghetti strap of her camisole off her shoulder, baring one mouth-watering breast. A small thump on the floor distracted him for a second, until the imperative that drove him resurged. But as he lowered his head to take her pouty nipple into his mouth, he saw the moiré-silk-covered box he had brought with him lying on the polished oak parquetry. Dimly he realized that with all the activity, it had worked its way out of his pocket.

He frowned, loath to turn his attention away from Gloria's glorious body, her inviting breasts, to that damned gold charm. But the reason he'd brought the gift penetrated the hot fog that controlled his brain.

Marriage should be forever. He had to make certain Gloria was the woman for him. And it had to be a choice made with his *head.* Only then should he consider taking her to bed—though lately he was finding it harder and harder to think of anything else. He vented a harsh breath. A shudder of frustrated need went through his body. He told himself over and over that making love to Gloria for the first time deserved preparation, romance, anticipation—wasn't that what women liked? She deserved better—much better—than an unplanned, explosive rut on her bed. She deserved to be wooed.

Reluctantly he smoothed the thin satin strap back over her shoulder. Her gaze followed his fingers' progress, but she offered no comment.

Another heavy sigh rasped through his throat. "I don't think we're ready for this."

"We aren't?"

Slowly he shook his head. "No. It ought to be really special the first time, don't you think? If we get to know each other a little better and—and feel we're right for each other... I mean it's just not—" He broke off, feeling like a damned fool. Right for each other? Hell, she seemed willing. That should be right enough. He ought to go ahead and tumble her onto the bed, pull off her pretty pants and open his jeans. A shudder rolled through him as he imagined what it would be like thrusting into Gloria, her long legs clenched around his naked hips.

With a will, Luke tore free of that incinerating fantasy. He took a deep breath and let it out, trying to reassemble his wits. "I'm not that kind of guy," he ended lamely, knowing he was exactly that kind of guy.

Gloria looked at him for a minute, then gave him a smile fit for the lips of an angel. "You're something special, Luke Cahill."

Feeling guilty and embarrassed, he bent to retrieve the jeweler's box. "Do you think we know each other well enough for you to accept my gift now?" he asked, offering it to her.

She blushed as she took his gift. "I would say so." When she opened the box, the faceted gold pig charm twinkled in the lamplight. The sapphire eyes winked. But now the charm came attached to a gold bracelet. "Wait a minute," Gloria protested. "There was no bracelet last time. This is far too expensive a gift—"

"Would you rather have a cheap bracelet?"

"No, but—"

"Then it's settled. You'll keep it."

"But why—"

"Because if I didn't give you something to fasten it to, I have a feeling I'd never have the pleasure of seeing you wearing your little swine charm."

She held out her wrist to him, and with a satisfied smile, he fastened the bracelet. "It's beautiful," she said simply. "Thank you."

Ten minutes later, she let him out through her front door. "I will be the hostess for your weekend with your Swedish guests."

Elation rose in Luke. "Really? I mean, are you sure?"

"Yes, I'm sure."

"All *right!*" He gave her a healthy kiss on the lips. "I guess sex and jewelry really do work."

Gloria gave him a smug smile. "No, they were just nice extras. I made my decision earlier this evening. I was going to call you tomorrow."

As Luke climbed back into his truck, he whistled softly. Things were looking good. Things were looking very good. Gloria was wearing his bracelet, and she'd agreed to be his hostess for the weekend at the lodge with the Adkissons.

Only one more test to go.

Chapter Eight

True to her word, Gloria helped Luke make the arrangements for the weekend with the Swedish business magnate
and his wife, then on Friday morning drove out to the lodge
to oversee the last-minute touches before Luke arrived with
his guests.

Now the nasal buzz of a small airplane grew louder, her-
alding Luke's arrival with the Adkissons. Quickly, Gloria
looked over the table the caterer had set for lunch, then went
to the bathroom, where she checked her hair and makeup.
She brushed her hand over the shoulders of her white camp
shirt, smoothed her khaki chinos, then slipped on a pair of
aviator sunglasses and left the house.

She drove the Land Rover over the primitive road to the
private runway surrounded by rocky hills, grass, sumac and
oak. Here, all one could usually hear was the sigh of a summer breeze and the occasional rustle of dry leaves. She
watched the King Air land then taxi toward her, knowing
Luke piloted the craft.

He opened the door and pushed out the drop-down stairs.
Fru Adkisson got out first. She was petite, in her mid-
forties, with short, fawn brown hair that framed her attrac-

tive, fine-boned face. She smiled as she descended the steps
to the ground.

Herr Adkisson followed. Gloria guessed him to be several years older than his wife. Of middle height and stocky
build, he presented the picture of robust health. His thick
gray hair gave him the look of an elder statesman.

Luke stepped close to Gloria and took her hand. Under
the cover of his other hand, he quickly, surreptitiously,
slipped a ring onto her finger. Confused, she looked down
to see that it was a simple gold wedding band.

"Fru Adkisson, Herr Adkisson," he said, "I'd like you
to meet my wife, Gloria."

His lie slammed into Gloria. Through her shock, she
heard the Adkissons' polite phrases, and somehow she
managed to respond. Her shock receded almost as quickly
as it had struck, and when it did, she wanted answers! But
before she could turn toward Luke, his arm encircled her
waist in a firm embrace.

"A pleasure to meet you," she said, despite the indignation bubbling inside her like hot soup in a kettle. Just what
was going on here? Luke hadn't said anything about pretending to be his wife when he'd asked her to be his hostess
for the weekend.

His fingers tapped her waist three times. What the devil
was that? she thought, fuming. Some bizarre code? She shot
him a piercing look, but the silvery, reflective lenses of his
sunglasses prevented her from reading his reaction—if he'd
even noticed. Again, his fingers pressed lightly against her—
three times.

Well, she wasn't about to make a scene right here. Her
training was too ingrained for that to be an option. Clearly
he wanted her to go along with him. She decided she would.
For the moment. At least until she got some answers—
damned *good* answers.

As the men unloaded the luggage and stowed it in the
Land Rover, Fru Adkisson confided to Gloria in excellent,
if accented, English, "I am happy that you are here. I feared
I would be the only woman."

Struggling to shove back her temper, Gloria managed a smile as all four of them climbed into the Rover. "We would never have done that to you."

Luke started the engine and headed toward the house, imparting bits of natural history along the way. He seemed too smooth, too assured for Gloria's liking. It didn't seem *fair* that he should be so calm after the bomb he'd just dropped on her head. She settled into her seat and seethed.

"This is very different, eh..." Herr Adkisson paused and seemed to search for a word. "Terrain. Very different from Sweden."

"Yes," Luke agreed. "Yes, it is. I know you've been here less than twenty-four hours, but what do you think of Texas so far?"

Not wishing the Adkissons to feel they'd been put on the spot, in case they hadn't fallen in love with Texas, Gloria turned to face them, glad for the distraction. "What was your first impression? We agree that our state must be quite different from Sweden." She gave them an encouraging smile.

"The people, they are very friendly, *ja?*" Fru Adkisson said.

Luke grinned. "Thank you."

Herr Adkisson considered a moment. "It is a little like Africa, I think."

Gloria could see nothing behind Luke's mirrored sunglasses, but she sensed his surprise.

"Africa?" he inquired. "How so?"

The Swede frowned slightly as if weighing his words. "Texas is more arid. More...brown. Soil. Hills. Plants. It is not so green as Sweden."

"Many areas of Texas are green, Herr Adkisson," Gloria said. "This is Hill Country, and at this time of year, things do turn a bit dry." Her mouth was saying all the right things, but her insides were in turmoil. She'd expected to act as tour guide, but she certainly hadn't bargained on playing house with Luke "All-I-Need-Is-A-Hostess" Cahill.

The ten minutes it took to get from the airstrip to the lodge seemed more like an hour. While the two men took the suitcases to the guest suite, Gloria took Fru Adkisson on a tour of the house. Who could resist the charm of the old stone-and-hand-hewn-log lodge? It came complete with a large fireplace in the generous living room, three bedroom-bathroom suites, a dining room adorned with a large antique oak table and chairs and a hundred-year-old chandelier made of stag antlers.

Finally, Gloria showed Fru Adkisson to the rooms assigned to the guests. "I'm sure you'd like a chance to rest and freshen up," she said. "A welcome luncheon is being prepared. A few Tex-Mex dishes, a few Swedish dishes. Will twelve o'clock be convenient?"

Herr Adkisson rose from the chair where he sat. "Yes, thank you, Mrs. Cahill. We will see you then."

Mrs. Cahill. As soon as she closed the door to their suite behind her, Gloria stalked to Luke's room next to it. She recognized her empty suitcase and some of her clothing piled on his sprawling king-size bed. Inflamed with righteous ire, she strode into her room at the end of the hall, where she nearly collided with Luke as he rushed out, his arms full of her toiletries and underwear. A white lace bra dangled from the bottom of his bundle.

"Just what do you think you're doing?" she demanded as he hurried past her down the hall to his room. She followed, hot on his trail.

"There, I think that's the last of it," he said, and brushed his door closed with his shoulder, still holding her toilet articles and lingerie. "And, please, lower your voice. We don't want them to think we're quarreling, do we?"

She stared at him in disbelief. Out of the corner of her eye, she saw her bra blatantly dangling. Gloria snatched it away from him. "Frankly, I don't care if they hear me," she said, lowering her voice to a furious whisper. "I want some answers, mister, and I want them *now*."

He dumped his burden onto the bed. Bottles and jars clinked together. Suddenly she realized she was standing alone with him in his bedroom. His potent presence heated every corner of the place, vibrating against her senses, humming under her skin. Instinctively she stepped back, as if that small distance could keep her free from the pull of his seductive net. She caught herself, annoyed with her cowardice.

"I didn't have time to warn you," he said. "Claire caught me on the car phone just before I met the Adkissons at the airport. Seems my intelligence on Herr Adkisson had been incomplete."

"Oh?" Luke's shoulders were so broad, so strong. His neck formed a marvelous, masculine column. Gloria struggled to break free of the net's relentless tug. She glowered, trying to concentrate. "Oh?"

"It seems Herr Adkisson is extremely—shall we say conservative?—on the subject of moral propriety."

"Moral propriety?"

He took a step toward her. "He's a fanatic about unmarried men and women staying under the same roof."

"The man is a *Swede,* for heaven's sake."

"Don't you think I know that?" Frustration bit each word.

"Swedes are probably the most open-minded people in the world," she said, waving an arm. The ends and straps of the bra flipped back and forth. She whipped her hand behind her back, out of sight. "Cohabitation without the benefit of matrimony is generally not considered a problem by them."

"Well, it is for our Herr Adkisson. Claire said my investigator just found out that year before last, Adkisson was a partner in a big co-venture." Luke raked his hand through his hair. "When he found out the other partner was living with his fiancée, all hell broke loose. I was just able to stop at a jewelry store on the way and get a pair of wedding rings." He held up his hand, showing off his own band. "Does yours fit?"

"Perfectly. You have one lousy spy, Mr. Cahill. I'd think a man in your position would hire only the best."

Luke began pacing. Sunlight through the wide picture window glinted now amber, now gold, in his mussed hair as he strode distractedly back and forth. "I hate this. Hate lying. Hate asking you to lie. Do you think I would, if there was any other way?"

Either Luke was telling the truth or he was a consummate actor, Gloria thought, observing him. As she studied the tension in his face, in his movements, her defenses softened. Perhaps he really did hate asking her to lie.

"You're a successful man. Is your business with Herr Adkisson really so important?"

"If it were just my business, I'd say no. But it's not. The American Children's Fund asked me to act as their representative in the negotiations for a tract of land in Florida where they want to build."

"The American Children's Fund?" she echoed. Her heart sank. Only the Grinch would stand in the way of that worthy organization achieving its goals.

Gloria's heart sank even further. "Don't tell me. Let me guess. They propose to build a Kids' Ranch on the land."

Luke held out his hands in supplication. "If there were any other way..."

"You know he'll eventually find out. What if we just explain? Tell him the truth? Then, if he still objects, I'll go home."

"Oh, he'll object, all right. You can bet on that. And where will that leave me? I'm pretty sure the caterer doesn't know Swedish customs."

"Well, if Herr Adkisson is such a successful businessman, wouldn't *his* spy have told *him* that you're a bachelor?" she reasoned hopefully, feeling as if she were being sucked into a swamp of lost battles.

Luke stopped pacing. "That occurred to me, so I came up with a story. We're newlyweds," he announced, clearly pleased with his inspiration. He looked at her, his summer blue eyes alight with hope. "Will you do it?"

"He'll find out eventually," she blurted, making one last desperate attempt to elude the disaster she foresaw. This weekend might well see the end to their good reputations, both business and personal.

Worse than that, she feared she might lose her heart.
Living as Luke's wife, even for two days... How empty the
rest of her life would seem.

"Maybe, maybe not. We'll worry about that later."

Gloria looked at him for a long moment, feeling like a
hunted fox who's gone to ground, only to find a cunning
hound waiting in her den. She released a heavy sigh. "Oh,
all right."

He swept her into his arms. "Thank you," he said simply, holding her.

"Hey, I'd like the kids to have their ranch, too," she told
him firmly, just so he didn't get any ideas about her mo-
tives. "I—"

His mouth stopped any other words she might have ut-
tered, stealing them away with tenderness. She melted into
him, slipping her palms up his warm, solid chest to grasp his
shoulders, whether to draw him closer or to gain some anchor in the giddy whirl that swept her common sense into a
spinning funnel, she couldn't say. Pliant and seductive, his
lips strayed from hers, moving up along her cheek to her ear.
His breath sighed softly on her skin. He caught her earlobe
gently between his teeth, sending a shaft of desire sizzling
through her. Her fingers curled into his unyielding shoulders. Against her she felt the hard proof of his arousal.

She tore away from him, alarmed at her own craving to
pursue this path. This insane path. It would lead right to
that big bed, now piled with her clothes.

"What?" Luke asked. "What is it, darlin'?"

Shaken by her deepening response to his touch, Gloria
took refuge in indignation. "*I* should be asking the questions here. You no sooner wheedle me into collaborating in
your outrageous lie, then you start...start..." She couldn't
say the words, couldn't allow her mind to call up the intoxicating sensory impression of Luke, of his heady evergreen-
and-male scent, of his strong body, of his lips.

"Start what? Kissing you?" He took a step toward her,
and she took a quick step back. "Holding you? Touching
you?"

"You did not touch me!"

"I did."

"You most certainly did *not*."

"What do you call what we were doing with our lips?"

"That was kissing," she said primly.

"Well, we damned well had to touch to do it. And you were touching me mighty closely, too. A man doesn't mistake the feel of a hot woman asking for more."

Mortified heat rushed to Gloria's face. Damn him! She had pressed into his body. She would have absorbed him into her every cell to keep forever, if that power had been within her reach. "I—I—"

"You liked it. The touching. You liked it every bit as much as I did."

"No gentleman would say such a thing."

Luke slowly stalked closer, closing the space she'd been stealthily putting between them. "But we both know I'm no gentleman, don't we? I'm a swine, remember? You wear the proof there on your wrist."

Suddenly the charm bracelet seemed to burn into her. It was evidence she couldn't hide. She lifted her chin. "I wear it because I think it's pretty," she said defiantly. She backed away from him, a step at a time, trying to maneuver the wide expanse of the bed between them.

"You liked it," Luke repeated, refusing to be side-tracked.

"All right! I liked it!" No denying how she had liked it. "There. Are you happy?"

He leveled a long, measuring look at her. "Yes. You see, I don't need to lie to myself."

She glared at him.

"Why do you keep pushing me away, Gloria?" he asked in a low voice.

"I believe we've had this conversation before."

"No. No, we haven't. We're a little beyond the first-date stage, and I think I've proved that I'm not the wacko you seemed to think I was—"

"I never thought you were a wacko. I just don't think we want the same things from life. This pretending-to-be-married situation certainly has done nothing to change my mind."

He muttered an oath. "We'll talk about this later. Right now, we've got to get you settled into this room. That is, of course, if you still wish to be my wife?" He raised a Viking's eyebrow.

Relief at not having to discuss their all-too-basic differences rushed through her. "I do." She cringed. Too late, she realized how her quick, unconditional agreement had sounded. "I mean—that is to say, I still plan to pretend I'm you're wife."

He turned away, toward the pile of her possessions on his bed, but not before she glimpsed his satisfied smile.

"First of all, we'd better put your stuff away." He nodded toward the dresser. "There are two empty drawers." Then he strode into the bathroom, and she followed, stopping at the doorway. "I guess we need more towels and things." His gaze found hers, delivering a searing charge of awareness that flamed across every nerve cell in her body.

The cool, tiled bathroom seemed suddenly warm and close. A panicky feeling seized her. What had she committed herself to? She'd be sharing a *bathroom* with this man. This irresistible, handsome, sexy man. Not a wise move on her part.

He raised his eyes, and she followed his gaze to the bed.

"No." The word was little more than a strangled croak, barely audible.

"We'd better get the bed cleared off."

"No," she managed more firmly. "I'm not sleeping with you."

"Not now, of course. Unless you want to take a little nap after we put away your clothes."

"Not ever. We are *not* sleeping in the same bed."

"We are unless you want to sleep on the floor."

"*Me?* Why not you? This was your brilliant idea. A gentleman would sleep on the floor."

Luke moved toward the bathroom doorway, and she scurried back into the bedroom ahead of him, eager to stay away from that dangerous magnetic pull of his. He went to the bed and began putting her clothes away. "We've already established that I'm not a gentleman. This bed is big enough for both of us. If you don't want to sleep with me, you'll have to find somewhere else to sleep as long as it's in this room."

Quickly she scooped up her lingerie and carried it to the dresser, where she made rapid work of arranging and folding, then tucking everything away into an empty drawer. She eyed the polished hardwood floorboards. She didn't want to sleep on the floor. "Do you have a rollaway bed?"

"No."

"A sleeping bag?"

"No."

"No sleeping bag?" she asked incredulously. "I thought this was a hunting lodge. Where's that pioneer spirit we all hear so much about? I thought hunters often used sleeping bags."

"Not when they have a comfortable lodge with nice, top-of-the-line mattresses."

So much for the pioneer spirit.

She scowled as she put a pair of shoes on the rack in the closet, deftly avoiding physical contact with anything belonging to Luke.

"Remember the orphans," he suggested.

"If you'll excuse me," she said stiffly, "I have to check on the last-minute details for lunch." Without waiting on his response, she hurried from the room.

Luke watched her go. This was supposed to have been an easy test. All he'd wanted was to see what kind of hostess she would make on a scale larger than an intimate dinner for two. But his test was backfiring.

He'd done everything he could think of to make this weekend a success. Last week, he'd called Ben Armstrong, the lodge's caretaker who lived in a bungalow on the edge of the property several miles away, and told him to put the lodge in first-rate order. He'd ordered a full report on Herr Adkisson. He'd even contacted the same caterers his family had always used for their weekends at the lodge. Though the company had recently undergone a change in ownership, the new proprietor seemed just as willing to make the long drive out to the remote location.

Because he'd determined, based on his information, that this land arrangement was going to be an uncomplicated affair, he'd figured that now would be a good time to conduct Gloria's final test. He flinched at the idea of testing her. God, he hated the whole concept, now that he'd come to know her better. But all he had to do was to think of his father and his brother, of sweet, innocent Poppy. Of the jeering he'd suffered from the other kids at school as he and Josh had been growing up. He'd been in countless fights over taunts about the trashy antics of his mother and the hangdog drinking of his father. Luke and Josh had sported black eyes more often than not, and had dealt out even more. Luke's nose had been broken three times by the time he graduated college.

And he remembered Barbara Tuttle. Try as he might, he'd never succeeded in wiping clean from his mind the image of her standing in the doorway of that small, dimly lit room upstairs at The Torchlight Club, where she worked as a waitress.

She wasn't supposed to be there. Only hookers used that room. But that's where he'd tracked her down. She'd just stood there in the doorway, her long, bleached-blond hair tangled and wild, her cheap rayon wrapper falling off one bare shoulder. He'd never seen her like that. Then the smell of stale cigarette smoke and liquor and recent sex struck him full in the face. Beyond her, on a shabby bedside table revealed in the faint hall light, lay two rumpled twenty-dollar bills and a half-finished drink. The jingle of a belt buckle drew his attention to the shadowy figure of a man pulling up his trousers.

Luke forced that memory back into the far recesses of his mind, wishing he could banish it forever. Just one more test. It wouldn't amount to much, considering how Gloria was already being tested more severely by pretending to be his wife. She was taking quite a risk. An unblemished reputation was important to her business. If word got out about this, there was no telling what could happen to her company.

Of course, if they were really married, what would anyone have to talk about? He glanced at his watch. Better ask Gloria what he could do to help her before the Adkissons came to lunch. Husbands did that, didn't they?

Pleased with that thought, he headed toward the kitchen.

Lunch went without a hitch. There had been no need to guide Luke around cultural pitfalls; the Adkissons seemed well versed in American customs. And the Swedes accepted Luke and Gloria as a married couple.

They were delighted with the Tex-Mex and Scandinavian foods that had been prepared. Fru Adkisson appeared to be the more daring of the two, sampling the spicy Southwestern dishes with gusto, taking only small portions of the pickled herring, the salmon salad, the stuffed cabbage and the other Scandinavian offerings. Luke politely served himself some of each, but Gloria sensed his lack of enthusiasm. Clearly, herring would never take the place of enchiladas in his affections.

After lunch, the men took the Land Rover and went out to bounce around the surrounding Hill Country, presumably to do a little male bonding before taking up the cudgels of commerce. Gloria enticed Fru Adkisson into a Western saddle on one of the lodge's riding horses—a big sorrel gelding—then swung up onto the back of an Appaloosa mare.

The two women meandered slowly through the rocky green-and-brown countryside around the lodge, discussing the different customs of their countries and the illogical ways of men. After twenty minutes or so, mindful of the fact that Fru Adkisson was not used to riding, Gloria suggested they dismount and walk to finish their outdoor tour.

It was dusk when they stabled the horses and strolled back into the house to discover that the men had arrived before them. After a shower, Gloria checked in the kitchen to see how everything was going. The caterer assured her that all was under control, and she joined Luke and the Adkissons in the living room. She passed out the glasses of chilled Chardonnay Luke poured.

They chatted companionably for a while, then went into the rustic dining room where the silent caterer served them dinner.

Gloria's appetite fled when she thought of spending the night with Luke. Only years of experience kept her smiling and conversing while her heartbeat hammered into triple time.

The gold band on her finger gleamed in the light from the antler chandelier. It was such a lovely ring. Odd that it fitted so perfectly. She found herself rubbing her thumb over the smooth metal.

It would be so easy to allow herself to believe this golden band really meant something, she thought wistfully. So easy and so very foolish.

She maintained her bright facade for the rest of the meal and through after-dinner coffee in the living room. All the while, the prospect of sharing a room with Luke Cahill nibbled at her nerves.

Finally the Adkissons said good-night and retired to their room, leaving Luke and Gloria alone.

Silently they walked down the hall and turned into Luke's bedroom. Gloria stopped a few steps past the threshold, her courage fading as she came face-to-face with the big four-poster. She heard Luke close the door behind them. The soft thud might as well have been the clang of prison bars crashing shut.

Luke came to stand behind her, and her heart roared into overdrive, beating so rapidly against her chest that she feared he would hear it. She had to get a grip on her reactions to him, she decided. It was important to act casual, as if their spending the night together was of no significance. As if his touch had never left her breathless and yearning. As if his kisses didn't send her into a dizzying maelstrom.

"Why don't you take the first turn with the bathroom?" he suggested. His breath warmed her nape, sending shivers through her. "Maybe a hot bath will help you relax."

She inched away from him. "What makes you think I'm not relaxed now?" she asked. "You go ahead. I—I'm a shower person anyway." A *cold* shower.

"As you like," he said. As he closed the bathroom door behind him, she glimpsed a satisfied smile curving his mouth.

She went to the chair, in which she proposed to spend the next two nights, and sat down. There was nothing on which to support her long legs. The back of the old leather chair came straight up at a ninety-degree angle, ending at an uncomfortable height. Disgusted, Gloria tried curling up. Her head jammed up against the square arm. Who had designed this thing, anyway? The Marquis de Sade? By morning she wouldn't be able to straighten her neck or shoulders.

She began to pace. No sleeping bags. No chairs but a ladder-back wooden number at the desk and that miserable leather instrument of torture. She'd been crazy to agree to pretend to be Luke's wife. Now she was trapped in a room with the man who could turn her insides to jelly with a single sultry glance, and with no bearable place to sleep. Insanity, that's what this was.

Through the wall she heard the sound of the shower running. Her footsteps faltered. He was in the shower. She came to a standstill. He was naked.

Naked and wet. His hard, long-muscled body would be streaming with water. His smooth, broad shoulders, his narrow hips and his firm, tightly curved buttocks would glisten with moisture. Diamond droplets would cling to the springy mat of amber chest hair, which narrowed in its descent down his taut, ridged abdomen—

Gloria wrenched her thoughts from their dangerous path. Desperate for activity, she rushed to her drawer in the dresser and dug out her nightgown. Her toiletries were already on the sink in the bathroom. They'd be all steamy by now, dripping with condensation like the mirror. Luke would be a tall, flesh-colored shadow in that mirror. Until he stepped out of the shower, closer—

Enough already! Gloria wanted to scream. Was there no escape from her one-track imagination? Her fingers clenched around her white cotton nightgown. Why hadn't she brought something more interesting? This thing was conspicuously dull. She sighed. Maybe wearing it would smother some of the sparks that seemed to be firing off in her body whenever Luke came near.

Suddenly the bathroom door flew open. Luke stood in the doorway, his hair dark gold and damp. He wore nothing but a pair of summer-weight sweatpants, which rode low on his hips. Gloria's mouth went dry. She was doomed. No woman on earth would be able to resist throwing herself onto the bed and dragging Luke Cahill with her. Only the fact that Gloria's feet seemed stuck to the floor and every muscle in her body was paralyzed prevented her from doing just that.

Luke stepped into the room. Without taking his gaze from her, he indicated the bathroom. "It's all yours," he said, his eyes sending a message that had nothing to do with a shower.

Gloria swallowed. Casual. She had to act casual. That would be the only way she'd make it through two nights with this man. "Thank you," she managed, and forced herself to walk, not run, into the bathroom. Once inside, she leaned back against the closed door and took deep, desperate breaths of the humid air. At last she straightened, hung her nightgown on the door hook and turned on the shower.

Luke lay on the bed and listened to the sound of the running water. How was he going to get through the night without touching her? Kissing her? Making hot, deep love to her?

He wasn't exactly sure why she was quite this upset over the situation, but until he could find out for certain, that was that. She might melt in his arms any other time, but not this weekend. Maybe she felt as if she was being rushed. Under normal circumstances, that would have been okay. He was a patient man. But to spend the night with Gloria without touching her, a man would have to be more than patient—he'd have to be dead.

At this very moment, only one thin wall separated him from her. She was standing in the same shower in which he'd stood, probably in the same spot. That thought brought a clutch to his gut. The water would have her all heated and rosy. Her head would be tilted back, exposing the sweet arch of her throat. Her slim shoulders would be slick with water, which would stream down her like ribbons of silver, down over her high, round breasts so ready for a man's lips, down over her belly, the curve of her thighs—

Luke thumped his head back into his pillow with a growl of frustration. Thinking about Gloria in the shower was *not* the way to help him get through the long hours ahead. Abruptly he sat up and got off the bed. He stalked to the leather chair and plunked down in it. If he was any kind of gentleman, he'd spend the nights in this chair.

He shifted around, trying to find a comfortable position in the unforgiving hulk of furniture. Damn, what were these springs made of? Stone? Try as he might, there was no comfort to be found in this chair. Either it was too small or he was too tall to come to any accommodation. With a huff of annoyance, he launched himself out of the chair. To hell with being a gentleman.

He began prowling the room. They were both adults. It was only two nights. This shouldn't be so hard. Luke glared at the big bed covered with handmade quilts. He shouldn't break into a sweat just thinking about having Gloria lying under the sheets next to him. He had to look at the big picture. Yeah, that was it. The big picture. Making love to Gloria would come in its own time.

Luke leaned straight armed against the massive post at the foot of the bed and studied the size and structure of the frame. The frame had been set up high so that a warming pan could be placed under the mattresses without catching fire. His grandmother had made the quilt with her own hands. Luke smiled. She must have spent a lot of time in this bed. His father had long ago told him that Grandpa and Grandma Cahill had made four of their six sons in this bed, and that two had been born here. Luke's smile faded. After Grandma Cahill died, Grandpa had gone a little crazy. Crazy like his sons, and their sons after them. But before that, he'd been married faithfully for almost thirty years to his first wife. Grandma Cahill must have been quite a woman to hold the heart of her man so completely that only death could separate them.

Luke wanted a love like that. He wanted a woman who could hold his heart as gently, as firmly, as Grandma had held Grandpa's. He wanted years of sharing the struggles and the triumphs. Of sharing the same bed, and of making babies who would grow up to someday look at this bed and think: That's what I want.

He turned to eye the closed bathroom door. Gloria was the one. He knew it. He could feel it in every fiber of his muscles and bones. But most of all, he felt it in his heart. With Gloria, he could make his life. She would share with him, encourage him, console him. And he would move heaven and earth to be her shield and her sword. When she hurt, it would be to him, Luke Cahill, that she would turn. To have this, he would willingly brave the fires of hell. Or two nights with Gloria without touching her.

Someday—soon—he would make Gloria his wife for real.

In the bathroom, Gloria stared horrified at her misty image in the large mirror. Dear Lord, it was worse than she'd feared—she was as dull as dishwater. In this nightgown she looked like a Victorian matron. Or a white tent caught in a high breeze.

She thought of Luke in his lightweight sweatpants and tried to remember why making love with him wasn't a good idea. It was always so much easier to think clearly when he wasn't around. But then, she wasn't sure just how long he would be around. And that was the real kicker. The one that punched her in the heart whenever she thought about it. She'd enjoy his company and his kisses for as long as she had him. When he realized that she just wasn't ever going to be any more exciting or exotic than she was now and went on to someone more dynamic, perhaps the rejection wouldn't hurt as much if she'd never given that last bit of herself to him. She touched the gold band Luke had slipped on her finger. Then she took a deep breath and opened the door...

To stare blindly into a dark bedroom. Blinking, waiting for her vision to adjust, she wondered if she'd taken longer than she'd thought, and Luke had simply decided to go to sleep. How flattering to know that spending the night with her wouldn't disturb his rest.

She flicked off the bathroom light, then groped her way to a window, where she parted the curtains. Moonlight flowed in, spreading its shadowed silver over carpet and furniture, and the long, still figure on the bed. An overpowering urge to observe Luke asleep sent her tiptoeing across the room to stand beside him.

In the light from the moon, his clean, classic features were cast into stark ink-and-mercury contrast. His thick lashes curved upon his cheek. His sensual mouth relaxed just enough to reveal the natural curved-up corners. Gloria smiled and reached down to brush back a stray lock of hair that had tumbled down over one eyebrow. Beautiful man. Her heart clenched at the thought of his leaving her behind. It was bound to happen, of course. Every other person of importance in her life had left her. Even Alice would soon, though not so definitely. When she married her Vern, it was only right that she devote her time and attention to him.

A deep, shuddering sigh escaped Gloria as she turned away to make her way to the chair. She was strong, she told herself. She could stand on her own. It was just... She curled up and laid her cheek against hard leather. It was just that standing on her own was so very lonely.

"Come to bed, Gloria," said a deep, drawling voice.

Her head snapped up to peer toward the source. "I thought you were asleep," she said indignantly, feeling betrayed and foolish.

"Obviously. Now come to bed. It's foolish for you to try to sleep in that chair. It's uncomfortable as hell." His voice softened. "Come on. I won't touch you if you don't want me to."

He wasn't the only one she was worried about. But he was right. This chair was miserably uncomfortable. She debated about it for a minute, then rose and, without a word, walked to the bed and got in, staying as far away from Luke as she could manage without falling off the edge.

"I don't bite, you know," he said peevishly.

She curled up in the covers, her back toward him. "It's not your teeth I'm concerned about."

She heard a rustle of sheets and turned to find that he'd raised himself on one elbow. "Are you implying that I've got no willpower?"

"I would never say a thing like that," she said, skirting his question.

"I think you just did."

"Well, I'm sorry if you took it that way."

"Yeah. Right." He pounded his pillow into a small lump, then lay back down.

Silence settled over the room, but she could tell by the rhythm of his breathing that he wasn't asleep. "I said I was sorry," she muttered.

"No, you didn't. What you said was, you were sorry that I was a jerk."

He was right. That's exactly what she had said, if not so nastily. She sighed. Luke Cahill was no jerk, but both of them were beginning to act jerklike. "I really am sorry."

"Apology accepted."

They lay side by side in the quiet room for several minutes. Gloria forced herself to close her eyes. Maybe counting sheep would help her to sleep. She called up a mental image of fluffy white lambs in a field. She urged them to jump over a wooden gate. One. Two. Three.

The sheets whispered as Luke shifted onto his side, his back to her.

Four. Five. Six.

She moved restlessly under the covers.

Seven. Eight. Nine.

The bed moved as Luke changed position again, but she determinedly kept her eyes closed.

Ten. Eleven. Twelve.

With a sigh, she rolled over onto her side, seeking a way to relax. Her bare foot brushed his bare foot. Quickly she moved hers, keeping her eyes squeezed shut. She could have sworn that this bed would have been a whole lot bigger than it seemed right now.

Thirteen. His warm breath fanned the top of her nose.

She opened her eyes to discover that she and Luke lay face-to-face. His eyes snapped open to find her staring at him. Seconds passed without their moving.

"I'm having trouble keeping my hands off you," he said, his voice low, little more than a rumble in his chest.

She heard each word clearly. Butterflies of delight fluttered in her stomach. "I'm glad to hear it."

One side of his mouth curled up. "I thought you would be, you little witch."

Gloria drew back a few inches on her pillow. "Witch?"

Luke softly traced her cheek with his forefinger. "You must be one, because you've cast a spell over me."

The butterflies beat their airy wings inside her. "I have?"

He nodded slowly. "Yes."

As she drank in the sight of his beautiful shadow-and-light face, he reached out and drew her to him. Knowing better, she allowed herself to go to him. He covered her lips with his and kissed her with such soul-wrenching tenderness that her throat swelled. A single tear rolled down her cheek.

Luke must have mistaken the cause of her tear. In the moonlight, she found concern in his eyes. "Have I hurt you in some way?" he asked.

She smiled for him. "No. You haven't hurt me." *Not yet.*

He came back for another kiss, this one more ardent. She felt his hand on her waist. Its warmth penetrated the thin layer of cotton to heat her skin. Her already weak will-power dived a notch. With trembling fingers, she removed his hand from her.

"Why?" he whispered.

Carefully, she chose her words, wanting to make him understand, yet needing to keep at least some of her pride. "I'm...I'm not a woman who can give herself lightly, Luke. I need to know a man is going to stay. For him to take my affections lightly, well, it makes me feel small. Unimportant. And it hurts a long time. I know this happens, so it's foolish for me to allow it, no matter how much I want to make love with someone. You see, for me, making love is something very important. It's...it's a testimony of faith. A *communion*. To have it taken with little regard beyond the moment is...unbearable." She searched his face. "I don't know what's in your heart, Luke, so I'm making no demands on you. In return, it's only fair that you make none on me." Her mouth quivered slightly as she tried to smile. "I'm only your pretend wife."

His gaze moved over her face. What was going on behind those moonlit eyes? she wondered. Finally he released a long, deep sigh. "I understand." A minute later, he turned onto his back. He folded his arms behind his head and stared up at the ceiling.

Disappointment sent the butterflies plummeting to a leaden heap in her middle. He understood—at least enough not to suggest a commitment. He was honest, she thought, rolling onto her side away from Luke. At least there was that.

In the morning, she woke to find Luke gone.

Luke knew who the footsteps belonged to without even turning around. It was strange how he seemed so attuned to her. But then, after last night, he knew Gloria Hamilton was the woman he'd been looking for.

It hadn't been easy for him to back off and leave her alone last night. Lying next to her in bed, hearing her breathe, knowing how satin soft she felt—minutes had dragged into hours and hours into an eternity. The little sleep he'd gotten had spun vivid, erotic dreams that had left him drugged with desire and not a little desperate.

Morning hadn't come soon enough, so while it was still predawn gray outside, he'd pulled on his clothes and boots and beat a quick, quiet path out of the room. But not before he'd lingered a moment to gaze at Gloria. Beneath her closed eyes had been bruised half-moons caused by lack of sleep. The sight had made him feel guilty, yet at the same time given him deep satisfaction. She'd wanted him as badly as he'd wanted her. Misery loved company, he guessed, and last night he'd been in a hell of misery.

He'd also known an elation he'd never felt before. Gloria didn't want just any man. She wanted one who would love her truly. One who'd be faithful to her. One who would respect her and her gift of trust.

That man was Luke.

The footsteps moved hesitantly across the kitchen toward him and the coffeemaker he was standing beside.

"Want some coffee?" he asked, not even turning around. Without waiting for an answer, he picked up one of the three remaining mugs and poured. Then he did move to face her, and his elation returned at the very sight of her. God, would she always affect him this way? Causing every protective instinct in him to rise up? Make him want to beat his chest and show off for her? He handed her the steaming mug.

"Good morning," Gloria muttered. She avoided meeting his gaze, and he refused to let her get away with it.

Gently he nudged her chin up, then planted a warm kiss on her pretty lips. "Good morning," he said.

Her eyes widened, and he saw in them the shadow of uncertainty. He smiled to dispel it, and to his relief she slowly smiled back.

His heart expanded. He intended to stay in her life. He would be faithful and patient and treasure her as no other man ever could. And he would tell her tonight.

The caterer walked into the kitchen. "I'll serve coffee in the dining room," he said, then began the bustle of preparing breakfast.

Luke winked at Gloria, then opened the swinging kitchen door for her to precede him into the dining room, where they found the Adkissons arriving.

The rest of the day passed in the company of his guests. Gloria had arranged a trail ride with a stop for a delicious picnic under an old oak. She coaxed the Swedish couple into showing off photographs of their children. *Someday that will be us,* Luke thought. Gloria and he would capture their own babies on tons of film and bore anyone who would listen with the details of their sons and daughters.

Finally the four of them gathered in the living room for drinks before dinner. Luke began to work the corkscrew into the bottle of the eleven-year-old Chateauneuf-du-Pape that would be served with the meal.

"We are having an American dinner tonight, yes?" Fru Adkisson asked when Gloria reentered the living room.

Gloria smiled. "Yes. Steak and potatoes."

Just as Luke extracted the dark, fragrant cork with a soft pop, the lights went out.

Chapter Nine

Fru Adkisson exclaimed in surprise.

"Please stay where you are," Gloria said. "Our eyes will adjust in a minute, and I'll be able to get a flashlight."

With the aid of the pale moonlight that spilled in through the window, she groped her way into the kitchen, where she heard the caterer swearing in a low, impassioned voice, and found her way to the drawer where she'd earlier seen a flashlight and several emergency candles. The flashlight came on with a nudge of her thumb. Leaving the caterer with a lit candle, she returned to the living room to find Fru Adkisson alone in the dark.

"They have gone to find another light and to check the generator," the older woman explained.

Fifteen minutes later, men's voices sounded in the hall, then another beam of light sliced into the room.

"Are you all right?" Luke asked. His flashlight lent his handsome face a demonic cast, throwing yellowish illumination up from underneath, creating stark, weird shadows.

Herr Adkisson came right behind him. "Viveka? Are you well?"

"Yes, Bergren. It is only dark in here."

"Dark and without power," Gloria said.

Herr Adkisson sighed. "Without power, there can be no dinner."

"It's the generator," Luke said.

By candlelight, Gloria refilled everyone's glass with wine. "What's wrong with it?"

Luke accepted his glass from her. "It doesn't work."

"Ah. I saw a gas grill outside. Why don't we just use that for the steaks and potatoes?"

"Excellent idea," Luke agreed immediately. "I'll go crank it up."

When Gloria informed the caterer of the new, necessary arrangements, the man bristled.

"The heat of a gas grill is very different from that of a broiler," he said stiffly.

"Yes, I know that." Gloria felt certain that Fred, her caterer, would never have taken such an attitude with a client. Luke had insisted that they use his own catering company, which had always handled the lodge's needs. "I'm afraid it can't be helped. The grill is all we have."

With a dark look that would have earned him dismissal if Gloria had had her say, the caterer muttered his assent and began readying the food for transfer outside.

Luke returned almost immediately. He was considering strangling Ben Armstrong. The man had always been dependable in the past. Damn it, Luke thought, he should have come himself to check out the lodge. He would have if there had been time. But there hadn't been, so he'd counted on Ben. Now what? Slap together peanut butter sandwiches? Hell, Adkisson was probably wondering what kind of incompetent Luke was.

"The grill's out of gas," he told Gloria, feeling like an idiot.

"What about the fireplace?" she asked. "It's a shame to waste good steaks."

The fireplace! Of course! Luke felt like grabbing her and kissing her. Conscious of his guests, he restrained himself. "It's early in the season, so Ben hasn't stocked any wood yet. But I could gather some now."

"It's worth a try."

He and Herr Adkisson spent an hour and a half gathering wood, and another thirty minutes chopping up the dead branches to fit the fireplace. When they got back to the house, he found the caterer had quit, packed up his gear and left. Vowing never to do business with that company again and silently cursing himself for a fool, Luke laid out the wood in the fireplace. Herr Adkisson opened the flue, then lit the fire and nursed it into a healthy, if smoky blaze.

"Mrs. Cahill is a versatile woman," he said approvingly as Gloria set the foil-wrapped potatoes in the fireplace, away from the fire. Then she strung the steaks on two long double-pronged forks and handed one to Fru Adkisson. They held them close to the flames.

"I don't know how this is going to work," she said, "but it's worth a shot."

What with the air-conditioning having gone off with the electricity and the fire crackling in the grate, the heat in the room grew stifling.

"Here," Luke said, reaching for Gloria's fork, "I'll take a turn at this. You go outside and get some fresh air. It's hot out, but not this hot."

She gave him a grateful look as she turned over her fork to him. Herr Adkisson took over for his wife.

Luke sat staring into the fire in an agony of embarrassment. This had never happened to him before. He'd built a reputation for efficiency, but Adkisson would probably never believe that now. The first time in Luke's life that he'd ever tried to mix business with something personal, and it had blown up in his face.

His only consolation was that tonight he'd again be sharing a bed with Gloria. He thought about holding her soft, womanly body close to his, about kissing her full, sweet lips. About—

"Fire!"

That one word snapped him out of his erotic daydream.

Gloria ran into the living room. "Fire! The roof's on fire!"

Throwing down the steaks, the men raced outside where Fru Adkisson stood wringing her hands, staring upward.

Sure enough, hellish yellow flames danced on the roof, bright against the black, starry sky.

"Gloria, hook up the hose," he shouted, then raced off to the stables to get a ladder. Herr Adkisson followed close behind him, holding on to the three buckets he'd managed to find.

By the time they returned to the back patio and set up the ladder, Gloria had hooked up the hose, but without the generator, the water quickly drizzled to nothing.

Luke scrambled up the ladder to the roof. Herr Adkisson followed, armed with a wet blanket.

The Swede smiled grimly. "I have always wanted to be a fireman."

Luke sprayed the spreading flames with a fire extinguisher. "It looks as if you're finally going to get your wish, Herr Adkisson," he said tightly as he watched the fire spread, fanned by the rare breeze. His great-grandfather had built the original portion of this lodge, and Luke had spent many wonderful boyhood summers here. There wasn't a fire department for a hundred miles.

"Bergren," Herr Adkisson said. "Please, call me Bergren."

"Bergren," Luke said, his eyes watering and smarting. He continued to spray the hungry flames with the small extinguisher kept in the kitchen as smoke blew into his face, nearly blinding him, burning his eyes and nose, choking him. Heat licked his skin. No matter how fast he laid down the foam, the fire seemed to move faster. The extinguisher gave out.

Bergren continued to beat at the fire with the heavy wet blanket.

"Luke!"

Luke whirled to find Gloria standing on the ladder, struggling to lift a full bucket of water onto the edge of the roof.

"What the hell are you doing up here?" he roared, snatching the bucket out of her hand. Without waiting for an answer, he ran to throw the water on the fire. As he turned back toward her, she heaved a sopping blanket up onto the roof for him.

"I'm helping to put the fire out," she said. "Viveka and I have already moved the horses out of the stable, just in case it spreads. With this breeze, it might."

"Thanks," he said as he snatched up the blanket and went back to work.

Several minutes later, Gloria returned. She slung another wet blanket onto the roof, and a sweating, hard-breathing Bergren traded the burned, smoking remnants of his blanket for it.

Gloria scrambled down the ladder, empty bucket in hand. "We've got to start a bucket brigade, Viveka. With no electricity, the pump isn't working, but there's still water in the horse trough." She thrust the empty pail into Viveka's hands. "Please, go fill this one. I'll get the bucket off the roof."

Viveka returned with a full pail and exchanged it for the two empty ones. Gloria hurried back up the ladder, balancing the full pail on her shoulder, holding it in place with one hand.

Luke took the water from her. Smoke had darkened his golden hair, which stuck out in all directions. His blue eyes were startlingly light against the sweaty mask of soot that covered his face. "We're making headway. Can you get some more blankets?" he asked, but he didn't wait for an answer, turning back to battle the fire.

An hour later, the four fire fighters sat on the patio, exhausted and filthy, taking thirsty swigs of the apple juice Gloria had retrieved from her pantry supplies. They had defeated the fire, but they couldn't accurately assess the damage, so it had been agreed the wisest choice was to return to Tidewater. Since there were no runway lights to guide the plane, everyone would have to pile into Gloria's old sedan.

She should have heaved a sigh of relief at learning she wouldn't have to spend the night with Luke in his bedroom, but even as that thought went through her mind, a pang of disappointment haunted her. Luke excited her like no other man she'd ever met before.

She didn't know where she stood with him, or even where he stood with her. Somehow, all her resolutions about not getting involved with him seemed to be slipping away. Until she could figure out exactly how she felt about him—aside from the fact that she was crazy about him—she knew she'd do better not to succumb to the desire that his searing gaze, his lingering touch, incited in her.

They all retrieved their belongings from the lodge, then Luke locked up the place. On the drive back, Luke dialed Ben Armstrong's number on the cellular phone, only to discover that Ben was in the hospital, laid low by a serious case of the flu. His thirteen-year-old granddaughter had tried to fulfill his obligations. Next he called White Oaks to have someone arrange for the care of the horses and security for the lodge.

When Gloria saw Bergren slap Luke companionably on the back, she suspected that a bond had grown up between the men. She certainly felt a lot closer to Viveka, whom she considered a newfound friend. The Swedish woman was a trooper, and Gloria felt lower than a worm, knowing that she and Luke had lied about their relationship.

She mentioned as much to Luke after they'd taken the Adkissons to an elegant Houston hotel and she was driving him home. A large, saffron hunter's moon glowed in the ebony sky. In the dark interior of the car, illuminated only by the faint lights from the dashboard control panel, she saw him slant her a look from the corner of his eye as he continued to face the road. Soot smudged his high, perfect cheekbones, his elegant jaw, his slightly crooked nose.

"We won't be lying for long," he said.

Relief filled her. "Do you plan to tell them the truth?" She wanted to be there when he did, so that she could make her apologies and explain to Viveka.

"I want to marry you, Gloria." He turned his head to face her then.

The sincerity she read in his eyes stunned her. "But— but—"

"You've got courage," he said, and she heard the admiration and pride in his voice.

"That's no reason to marry someone!"

"No. But it's a reason you might take a chance on me."

"Take a *chance* on you? Luke, you'd be taking every bit as big a chance as I would. You're a prince in Tidewater, one of the reigning families. I'm almost a newcomer here. What do you know about me except that I teach etiquette and protocol for a living?"

After she pulled into his driveway and switched off the ignition, Luke turned to her, pinning her in her seat with the intensity she found in his handsome face. "I know you're a real lady," he said, his voice low.

She swallowed hard. "Is that so important to you?"

"Yes. But that's not all. You like kids. You're also warm and intelligent, and you don't hesitate to stand up to me." He lifted his hand to cup her cheek. His voice dropped to a husky, sexy rumble. "You're lovely and sweet."

Tears tightened her throat, burned at the backs of her eyes. "Such flattery."

"Such truth."

She yearned to press her cheek against his palm, to curl up in his arms and let tomorrow take care of itself. But she couldn't. Some elusive sensor, deep within the region of her heart, told her that Luke wanted her for all the wrong reasons. He might honestly believe that she was warm and intelligent and brave. Maybe even that she was pretty and sweet. What came filtering through, though, was the importance he placed on the fact that she was well mannered and that she liked children. The first reason was anathema to her. The second reason just wasn't enough.

Gloria straightened, pulling away from him. She fought for a smile. "We're both tired. Now is not a good time to discuss anything important."

He looked at her for a long moment. Then he got out of the car and unloaded his garment bag and briefcase, carried them inside and set them in the foyer.

Then he turned and took her into his arms. He smelled of smoke and earthy male sweat. Ash dimmed his usually bright hair. "I won't take no for an answer," he murmured. His lips brushed over hers, tasting faintly of salt, before settling down to a deep, open, passionate kiss that magically swept away the past hours. It tilted her equilibrium and sent her blood singing through her veins. Her hands instinctively sought him for balance, smoothing over his ribs, sliding around to his back. Hot and moist, desire curled deep inside her. Her fingers tightened convulsively.

He stepped back, leaving her dizzy and breathless and thoroughly aroused, as only he had ever managed to do. His nostrils flared with his every shallow, explosive breath.

"I'll pick you up tomorrow for breakfast with the Adkissons at their hotel," he said, his deep voice husky.

She nodded, then watched dazedly as he strode into his house. The most eligible man in Tidewater had just asked her to marry him.

Maybe for all the wrong reasons.

She came back for breakfast with the Adkissons the next morning, continuing to be a good "wife." Afterward, Luke gave her a husbandly kiss and asked her to take the Mercedes "home." Looking forward to a visit with Maudie, Gloria obliged.

The maid answered the door and showed Gloria into the kitchen, where Maudie was wrist-deep in bread dough.

"Well, look who's here," Maudie said, her face lighting in welcome. "Please, pull up a chair and visit with me. What would you like to drink? I just made a fresh pot of coffee."

Gloria accepted the offer. After the maid served the coffee, she left the kitchen.

"I do hope you'll forgive me," Maudie said, vigorously kneading the bread dough on the long oak worktable, "but I'm at a place I can't stop now or it will be ruined."

Gloria took her coffee around to the other side of the table so that she could talk more companionably with Maudie. "I guess Luke told you what a fiasco the weekend turned out to be."

Maudie laughed. "You really had a time of it." Her hands pounded and slapped the pale brown, malleable mass. "The power going out, the grill running out of gas, the fire. Poor Ben nearly had a relapse when he found out what had happened. The man really is conscientious, and his granddaughter is the sweetest little thing. She'd do anything to please her grandpa."

Gloria smiled. "I guess she just wasn't up to being a chimney sweep or a generator mechanic."

"It does seem so, doesn't it? Well, all's well that ends well. And Luke certainly believes you outperformed all expectation—" Maudie abruptly broke off. Bright pink bloomed in her cheeks as she kept her gaze glued to the dough.

A suspicion that something was going on that Gloria hadn't realized began growing inside her. Maudie clearly felt she'd said too much. Gloria set her cup down on the counter. "Pardon? Outperformed? Just what was expected of me?"

Maudie finally looked up, but the color remained. "It's just that..." Her voice faded. Her gaze slid away. The woman was hopeless at lying.

Gloria studied the other woman intently. "What is it, Maudie?"

Maudie's hands stilled. "Do you love him?"

Oddly, that question had never arisen. Luke had never inquired.

Gloria met Maudie's gaze. "Yes. I love him." Even as she spoke the words, they seemed too paltry, too insignificant to describe the undeniable, somehow magical bond that connected her to Luke. If only he could feel the same way about her.

"I've seen the way Luke's been behaving lately, and there's no doubt in my mind that he cares deeply for you," Maudie said. "But the boy's been hurt too many times not to be cautious."

Suspicion prickled along Gloria's back. "Has Luke been...testing me?"

Maudie went back to work on the dough, keeping her eyes trained on it. "Could be that he has," she muttered.

That bit of news surprised Gloria. "He has the reputation for being unpredictable. I'm always reading and hearing about how some unexpected move of his has thrown his competition off."

Maudie thumped at the dough as if it were a punching bag and she an edgy boxer. "That's business, dear. There's a big difference with Luke. In his business ventures he's always been willing to take calculated risks. But not with his heart. With his heart, he's very careful."

That detail clicked into place in Gloria's mind. *Luke certainly believes you outperformed all expectation.* Maudie hadn't been speaking in the abstract. Gloria had actually been performing within parameters Luke had constructed. The thought was like a knife thrusting into her heart. "The barbecue was a test," she said dully.

"As I recall, that was your first date together. All first dates are tests, dear."

Gloria began to pace the length of the large kitchen. "That's true, but usually they aren't structured, they aren't so—so *calculated*." She stopped. "Tell me, did you start planning that barbecue before or after Luke invited me?"

Maudie hesitated. "After."

Gloria's stomach churned with disappointment and anger. "If the barbecue was to see if I liked children—"

"And if you could get along with his family, I'd think."

"Then what was the second date? He manipulated me into inviting him to my place for dinner. Did he want to check out my homemaking skills?" Realization struck with sickening force. *You're a great hostess.* "He wanted to make certain I know how to entertain properly." Gloria swallowed hard. "He's making sure that I have the taste to choose correctly." An ugly thought occurred to her, but when she tried to push it away, it boomeranged back. The facts were all there if one knew in what order to assemble them. Her eyes widened with stunned surprise. "My God, he's trying to make certain I'm not a bimbo!"

Maudie's forehead puckered. "Now, Gloria dear, don't go jumping to any conclusions—"

"He is. You know he is." Gloria glared at Luke's aunt.

The crimson flush that colored Maudie's cheeks furnished the answer.

"How dare he!" Righteous fury burned inside Gloria like a white flame. She wanted to throw something, to break something. She needed to hear the discordant tinkle of broken glass, the crash of splintering wood, the solid thud of a certain male body hitting the ground.

"We don't know anything for sure," Maudie offered, attempting to soothe.

"I can damned well put two and two together." That arrogant swine had been testing her all along! "And he told me he liked my fanny," she muttered, the soblike catch in her voice infuriating her even further. She would *not* cry over the likes of Luke Cahill. He didn't deserve her tears. Not a single one of them.

Gloria drew a ragged breath. Her anguish flooded in, convulsing in her chest, pressing on her lungs.

Maudie's eyes glistened with sympathy. "Luke wouldn't ask you to marry him if he didn't love you."

"I don't doubt that Luke loves someone," Gloria said. "But I'm not sure if it's me or the perfect hostess."

Chapter Ten

Throughout the next three days, while Luke was in Austin with the Kids' Ranch people, Gloria thought about his tests. The more she thought about them, the more hurt and infuriated she became. But the man had asked her to marry him, and deep in her heart, Gloria believed Luke must care for her. Surely the lightning between them, the laughter and the joy, could not be faked. And she loved him. Maybe . . . maybe it wasn't that he wanted a hostess as much as he didn't want a bimbo. Why did he have such a grudge against women with liberally applied makeup and too-short skirts? Fashion discretion, etiquette and good grammar could all be learned. Every one of the Cahill wives in Gloria's class was living proof of that. All it took was opportunity and motivation. She was the opportunity; the love these women had for their husbands and their children was strong motivation. Who couldn't admire the determination of these women to fit into their husbands' world?

Apparently Luke.

Gloria drummed the end of her pencil on her desk blotter. Well, she wasn't a so-called bimbo, but she did love Luke, so she'd worry about that problem another day. Right now, the little matter of his testing her needed to be addressed. He must never do that again, and the only way she felt she could impress that on him for all time was to give him a taste of his own medicine.

So Thursday night, when she checked her watch, she smiled. Ten o'clock. Time for The Test. She'd spent no little time devising what she considered a suitable trial for her macho beloved. He was about to learn that his perfect hostess had another side to her.

She dialed White Oaks, where Maudie answered, then called Luke to the phone. Gloria endeavored to sound distressed. "Luke, I'm so sorry to call you at this hour, but I need your help."

"What is it, darlin'?" Concern rode his voice.

She struggled with a moment of guilt. But he had to be made to realize how his tests had made her feel. It must not happen again.

"I have a ring," she said. "It's very precious to me. I—I took it off to rinse a few dishes and..."

"And what?" he coaxed soothingly.

"It fell down the drain," she wailed. "I'm sure it's caught in that little curly pipe under the sink, but I can't get to it."

"The P-trap. Did you call a plumber?"

"N-n-no," she said hesitantly. "I called you." She batted her lashes at Hamlet, who perched on his stand and cocked his head at her, as if trying to understand his human's strange behavior. She rushed on breathlessly. "I mean, you know all about plumbing, right?"

"Uh, right."

"Will you help me? Please, Luke." She held her breath, hoping he would agree. If he told her to call a plumber, she'd have to come up with a new test.

"Just let me collect some tools, and I'll be right over," he said firmly.

"Oh, thank you. I knew I could count on you."

After she hung up, she walked to the kitchen sink and dropped a ring down the drain.

* * *

Even as Luke gathered the tools he thought he might need, a quiet, annoying voice at the back of his mind pointed out that he was nuts to attempt tearing apart Gloria's pipes and putting them back together. What did he know about plumbing, anyway? Nothing. He'd never learned to be a handyman. Instead, his education had focused on those skills that would make him enough money to afford the services of experienced professionals when they were needed. He scowled as he examined a pair of wire cutters, then tossed them into the toolbox he planned to take with him. So he'd never tackled kitchen pipes before. So what? Gloria thought he could do the job, and he wasn't about to miss an opportunity to look good in front of her. If she thought plumbing was a manly genetic thing, then he'd damned sure do his best to at least get her ring back for her. How hard could it be?

Forty-five minutes after her phone call, he knocked on her door, toolbox in hand. He tossed off a casual salute when she answered. "Ever-Ready Plumbing Services," he said with a smile. He thought she looked cute and sexy in those cutoff jeans and that shirt tied under her dream-inspiring breasts. She ought to wear her hair in a ponytail more often.

"I'm so glad you're here," she said as she stepped into his arms.

There in the light of the amber porch lamp, Luke cradled her luscious body close to his, proud that she thought him so capable of saving her precious ring, pleased that she believed him capable of taking care of her. A swell of determination rose in him. He'd make things right for her. He wanted her to continue to turn to him.

Slanting his mouth across hers, he claimed her with a scorching kiss. She was his. *His.* Soon he would persuade her to realize that. Then she'd stop this dithering around and marry him.

"No, no, no!" crowed Hamlet, waddling through the entrance hall toward them.

Gloria sighed as she scooped Hamlet up on the back of her hand. "You know he has to say his piece, too. I've never seen him take such a liking to anyone other than me. Surely it's a good sign. Sometimes animals sense things." She led Luke into the house to the kitchen.

He went to the sink, where he found she'd emptied the cabinet below and laid out a clean cloth for him to lie on. "I've heard that dogs, maybe even cats, sometimes sense things about people," he said, "but I can't recall ever hearing it said about birds." He set down his toolbox.

"Maybe so," Gloria said, rubbing her cheek against the conure, who preened. "But as you well know, Hamlet is a very special bird."

Luke had to smile as he watched his woman and her small companion. "Yes, he is a special little fellow at that."

Hamlet studied Luke for a minute, directing first one beady black eye, then the other, toward Luke. "Good night, sweet prince!"

"Sounds like a suggestion to get to work," Luke said. He squatted on his heels in front of the cabinet. The P-trap lurked in its shadowy interior. "I need a flashlight," he told Gloria, who promptly retrieved one from a drawer and handed it to him.

Rust speckled the old metal pipes and encrusted their fittings. He licked suddenly dry lips. This might not be as easy as he'd thought. "Do you have a bucket?" he asked, thankful to be able to think of anything useful. "There's bound to be some water standing in the pipes."

As soon as she left to go find a pail, he quickly clamped a wrench into place on the fitting that attached the P-trap to the drainpipe from the sink, and pushed. Or tried to. The wrench didn't budge. He tried again, harder. Again, the fitting held firm. He scowled as he studied it. For being old and rusty, it seemed pretty damned strong. Maybe NASA should try building their rockets out of this stuff.

"Here's the bucket," Gloria said.

Startled out of his speculations, Luke banged his head on the garbage disposal unit. He gritted his teeth. "Thanks."

"How is it coming? Can I get you anything? What about a nice cool drink? Do you think there's a manual for these pipes? If there is, I might have it somewhere."

Seeing a chance to get rid of her for a while so that she couldn't witness his ignorance firsthand, he seized on her offer of a drink. "How about a nice, tall, cold—" he searched his mind for something she'd be unlikely to have "—guava juice."

She leaned down, peering at him through the open cabinet door. It gave him the most insecure feeling, lying there on his back, the top quarter of his body surrounded by the dark interior of the cabinet, the underbelly of an old iron-and-porcelain sink hanging directly above his face. "Guava juice?" she asked. "I don't have any."

"Oh." He wriggled out from under the sink only to come up close and personal with the long, silken length of her bare legs. He swallowed hard and tried to remember what he'd been about to say. "Uh, that's okay. I mean, if you don't have any." He lifted mournful eyes to meet her gaze. "I understand."

"Well, I'll go get some," she offered immediately. "It's the least I can do."

"Are you sure it's not too much trouble?" This is pitiful, he thought. How had he gotten himself into this mess?

"No, no. There's a Quickie Mart just a half mile down the road. I'll bet they have guava juice. But if they don't, do you have a second choice?"

"Kiwi tea."

She looked as if she was trying to decide whether or not he was really serious. Luke carefully schooled his features to reflect hopefulness. *Really pitiful.*

After she'd gone, he went directly to the phone and got Josh on the line, hoping to extract some useful information. When he explained the situation, and Josh finally stopped laughing, all Luke learned was that his brother knew even less than he did about plumbing. Disgusted, Luke crawled back under the sink. He set his wrench in place and tried again. And again. The second time something tightened painfully in his shoulder. He swore vilely, but continued to twist away at the fitting.

He felt a light pressure on his foot and looked down to find Hamlet perched on the toe of his sneaker. The little conure tilted his head. Gazing calmly at Luke, Hamlet repeated two of the worst words that had escaped Luke's lips.

Luke stared at Hamlet in consternation. Great. He'd taught foul language to the beloved pet of the woman he was trying to impress. Well, that would impress her, all right. But she'd be even more surprised if she got home with his damned guava juice and found he'd accomplished nothing. He went back to work. He threw all the power of his upper body behind the wrench, and—finally—he felt the coupling give.

Hamlet hopped down from his white-sneaker perch and waddled confidently up the length of Luke's supine body. "No, boy," Luke ordered sternly. "Down. Down, boy." But Hamlet kept coming, oblivious to the absence of welcome. *"Stay,"* Luke commanded.

Hamlet halted. The conure cocked his head, solemnly studied Luke's face and let out another expletive.

Luke groaned and lay back down. Oh, yeah. Gloria was really going to appreciate that.

Under his wrench, the fitting moved grudgingly, but he managed to twist it almost all the way off. Then he rescrewed it just enough to hold that end of the trap in place while he attacked the fitting that secured the other end, which was attached to the pipe that disappeared into the hole in the wall.

After much sweat and several stifled oaths, he felt the second fitting loosen. A second later, he heard the front door open and close.

"Hello," Gloria called, "I'm home." He heard the rustle of a paper bag, then saw her shapely, bare legs round the corner and walk toward him.

Hamlet didn't leave his place on Luke's abdomen, but his small feet beat a tattoo as he turned around to greet Gloria. "No, no, no!"

"How cute," Gloria said, laughter bubbling below the surface of her voice. "A man and his bird." She bent to look inside the cabinet. Her ponytail flipped down to rest along her cheek. "How are you doing, plumbing master? Are you ready for your kiwi tea?"

He smiled up at her, trying not to feel like a belly-up turtle. "What? No guava juice?"

Gloria lifted an eyebrow and favored him with a look of mock severity. "You'll drink kiwi tea and like it. I went to two stores. Neither had guava juice, and only one had kiwi tea. A single bottle."

"Kiwi tea is good."

"I'm glad to hear it."

As she prepared his drink, he separated the rusty trap from the arrangement of pipes, then quickly placed the bucket under them. Careful not to tip the trap, Luke scooted out from under the sink. Giving up at last, Hamlet fluttered over to his perch.

"You've found my ring," Gloria exclaimed as she saw the trap in Luke's hands.

"Well, no, not yet." He took the thing outside and, with the help of the garden hose, carefully emptied the grungy contents onto the concrete pad of her back step. An unpleasant odor wafted up. She squatted next to him and watched as he sorted through the mess with the tip of a screwdriver.

"There it is." She pointed to a dull gleam of gold.

Quickly, Luke rescued her ring and rinsed it off. "This is it?" He stared at the junky piece of plastic in his palm. Little of the gold paint remained. It looked like a trinket from a box of really cheap cereal. "This is what you called me at ten o'clock at night to come fetch? I thought it would have at least a diamond or two on it."

Gloria whisked the ring from sight, stuffing it into the pocket of her shorts with barely a glance. "Sorry. No diamonds."

Before he could say anything, she went back inside. Baffled by her strange behavior, Luke washed off the back step and put away the hose, then followed her inside.

"What's going on?" he asked.

She handed him a tall, frosted glass of darkish green liquid. Ice cubes tinkled musically. "Doesn't the gizwhichy have to go back on the pipes?" She vaguely waved her hand in the direction of the trap.

Luke scowled. He knew a bum's rush when he got one, and he wasn't having any of it. "I thought that ring was so all-fired important to you, but you've barely glanced at it."

"I know what it looks like. It doesn't look any different now than when it fell down the drain."

"You don't seem particularly glad to get it back," he muttered into his glass.

She gave him a quick, sisterly peck on the cheek. "Thank you, Luke. I do appreciate it."

His scowl didn't go away. Now he really was sure there was something wrong. He'd never before received such a chaste kiss from Gloria. He didn't like the feel of it. Not one bit. But because he wasn't certain what the matter was, he got back under the sink and screwed the couplings in place, securing the trap.

"All done?" she called from above him. "Is it all right if I use the faucet?"

"Yeah." He inched out of the cabinet and sat up. She handed him a tea towel on which to wipe his hands, then turned on the water. It poured out from around the top coupling on the trap.

"Stop!" Luke shouted as he shoved the bucket under the waterfall. "Shut off the water!" She complied immediately.

He trained the beam of the flashlight on the pipe and leaned close to inspect it. He found a crack.

She hunkered down next to him and studied the rust-flecked mass of tubing. "What happened?"

"A crack in the pipe," he said glumly. Oh, yeah. This was the way to look good in front of his future bride. Tear up her kitchen. "Must've happened when I was trying to loosen the coupling."

They sat on the floor, side by side in silence for a moment, looking at the damage. Finally, Gloria spoke.

"How does it feel?" she asked.

"Huh?"

Her level gaze met his, and somehow, in that eternal second, he knew he'd been set up.

He rose, hot with indignity and embarrassment, confused by the hurt he felt. "You never cared about that ring, did you? This—this—" he waved his hand at the wet towel, the sopping cloth, the bucket, his scattered tools "—was nothing but a joke to you."

"It was no joke, Luke." There was something about her calm, her poise, that he found annoying, unnerving.

"Look, I don't know why you felt the need to make me look like a jerk," he said coldly, "but I'd appreciate a few answers. Why the hell did you drag me here when it's obvious you don't give a sh—" He broke off with a quick glance at Hamlet, who now perched serenely on his stand just inside the kitchen door. "You don't care about that ring." Luke's jaw tightened.

Through his growing anger, Gloria's words came back to him. *How does it feel?* He cut her a sharp look. No. It couldn't be. But there it was in her eyes.

She knew.

A sick feeling coiled in Luke's gut as he stared into Gloria's lovely, clean-scrubbed face, into her knowing brown eyes.

How does it feel? she'd asked, and now he knew why. Somehow she'd learned about the way he'd tested her. He tried to imagine how she'd felt when she'd found out. It didn't take much effort. If her humiliation, her anger and her hurt had come even close to what he'd been feeling a moment ago, it was too much.

"It doesn't feel good," he said, his voice low and rough.

She searched his face, clearly taking no pleasure in her triumph. "No, it doesn't, does it? You feel... betrayed...don't you?"

"Yes." God, yes.

She looked down at her hands, which rested on her knees. "It is a betrayal. We may not trust all our feelings toward each other, but for some reason, I think we've come to trust each other as people." He saw her throat work. "Trust is

such a rare, a *precious* thing, a kind of...miracle." She
stood up. "I trusted you, Luke. I might not have trusted
myself where you were concerned, but I trusted *you*. And
then I found out I was nothing but a rat in a maze to you."

"That's not so," he denied vehemently, taking a step toward her, instinctively reaching for her.

She took a step away from him. "I think you should go
home now," she said. "Think about the way you feel. This
was just one little test, and I told you about it at the end.
Consider how I must feel, knowing that what I thought was
a special relationship was just a series of tests." She drew a
sharp breath and huffed it out. Moisture glistened in her
eyes. "Go home, Luke."

The next day, Gloria didn't hear from Luke. She wondered how she managed to act as if everything were normal
when her whole life seemed to be crumbling around her.
Intellectually she knew that it wasn't, of course. She still had
a successful business. She had friends.

No, it wasn't her life that was crumbling. Just her heart.

She sighed raggedly as she shuffled papers aimlessly from
one pile on her desk to another. She'd known the risk she
was taking when she'd put Luke through his test, but she
didn't see how she could have handled things any differently. He'd needed to know how he'd hurt her, or there
might have been more tests.

Well, maybe he was thinking it over. Maybe he was
struggling to come to grips with his guilt. Ha. Not likely.

She'd expected a certain satisfaction when she'd let him
know that he'd just been tested. But as he'd stood there in
her kitchen, his hair mussed, a smear of rust on his cheek,
his clothes drenched and stained, the embarrassment and
hurt in his eyes had robbed her of her triumph.

Alice rushed into her office. "Luke's on the telly!"

Gloria hurried after Alice into the tiny break room, where
an old portable television sat on the far end of an even older
kitchen table.

"...a member of Tidewater's reigning family," the field
reporter was saying. "When we contacted Daniel Cahill re-

garding the arrest of his son, he refused to comment.'' The view on the screen was of a media madhouse on the steps of the Sharlow County Jail. The camera zoomed in on Luke getting out of a patrol car, his hands cuffed behind his back. His beautiful face showed no emotion. His dark T-shirt and jeans, his black tooled-leather belt and Western boots, his hard-muscled leanness all combined to give him a dangerous look. He turned and glared at a reporter who darted forward to shove a microphone in his face. A sheriff's officer ordered the reporter back, then took Luke's arm, as did an officer on the other side of Luke. The three strode swiftly into the station through the crush of gawkers, reporters and cameramen.

Horrified, Gloria watched. ''What's the charge?''

''They say he bribed Commissioner Newton Lockington, that they have evidence.''

''It's a lie,'' Gloria declared hotly. ''Luke would never bribe anyone.''

She imagined how Luke must be writhing inside at being trapped in the public eye, his hands in cuffs like a common criminal as he was herded into the county sheriff's station. The media would have a field day with the one Cahill who'd managed to keep his life reasonably private.

As the TV camera focused on the glass front doors to the building's marble-tiled lobby, Gloria and everyone else in Tidewater could see one of the officers speaking briefly with Luke, who nodded. The deputy removed the handcuffs. Rubbing his wrists, Luke walked with the officers to a bank of elevators.

Suddenly Lockington appeared, surrounded by an entourage bristling with microphones and camcorders, and the view on the television screen switched to inside the lobby.

Newton Lockington, a portly, balding man of medium height, wore an expensive suit and a smug smile.

''Well, Officers,'' he drawled loudly, ''I'm glad to see you've apprehended this criminal.'' He shook his head sadly, clucking his tongue. ''Of course, the Cahills have always been a troubled lot, but to my knowledge, none of them has ever attempted to bribe a public official before today. It would seem the one *good* Cahill has turned out to be notorious.''

Luke lunged forward, grabbing the commissioner by the front of his shirt. ''You sorry son of a bitch,'' Luke snarled, giving the frightened-looking man a shake. The two offi cers surged around Luke and dragged him away from the panicked commissioner. ''Leave my family out of this,'' Luke shouted over the commotion. ''You framed me. You stole my check and framed me, but your time is coming. You're going to fall hard, Newton.''

Hastily, Lockington brushed at his rumpled shirt. ''We'll see who falls, Cahill.''

The elevator doors opened, and the sheriff's men hustled Luke inside. The view of the lobby vanished, replaced by the face of the anchorwoman.

Gloria ran back to her office and grabbed her purse. ''Cancel my appointments, Alice.''

''Give him my best, dearie. Tell him we know he's inno cent.''

Forty minutes later, Gloria was admitted to Luke's cell. His belt was gone, his hair was mussed and a bruise was swelling and darkening under his eye. He rose from the narrow cot as soon as he saw her. She went directly into his arms, and he clutched her fiercely for a minute, saying nothing, his face buried in her hair next to her temple. She felt his heart pounding rapidly, felt his ragged breath warm against the top of her ear.

''I don't believe a word of it,'' she said. ''The man's ly ing through his teeth.'' She reached up and lightly touched her fingertips to his cheek, just below the bruise. ''What happened to your face?''

Luke's mouth curled up in a wry smile. ''I 'fell' when they were taking my belt from me. Seems Newton's got some buddies here on the force.''

Alarm flared within her. ''You can't stay here. It isn't safe for you. Where is your lawyer? He should have been here immediately!''

Luke hushed her softly, cradling her against him, stroking her hair. "Don't you worry, sweetheart. Josh was here earlier and told me that my attorney is on his way."

Gloria clung to him. "I'll stay with you until he gets here," she said, furious at Lockington, and his thugs, worried for Luke. "If you have a witness, they won't dare harm you again."

He went still. It frightened her.

"You can't stay," he said, his deep, drawling voice low, barely audible.

"If they try to make me go, I'll make a scene," she vowed, coming up with the worst thing she could think of—a public display. "I'll scream and kick." She held him more tightly. "They can't make me go."

Luke straightened slowly, easing her away from him, his hands firm around her upper arms. His gaze moved over her face as if he was memorizing her every feature. "You can't stay, Gloria. I can't let you."

She found it hard to breathe. "You don't want me here with you?" She'd feared she might have driven him away. It seemed she had been right.

He looked away. "It's not that."

She searched his face for some clue of what was going through his mind—and his heart. His shuttered expression defeated her. "Then tell me what it is. Is it . . ." Her voice died away, and she swallowed dryly. "Is it because of last night?"

"No." He rammed his fingers through his hair. "God, no."

"Then what?" She hated the tears that thickened in her throat, the pleading note that robbed her words of their strength.

His beautiful mouth twisted. "I'm poison to you."

She shook her head violently. "No. I love you."

"Don't you understand? No decent woman is safe with a Cahill."

"That's ridiculous!"

"What's ridiculous is your insistence on dragging your name through the dirt." He released her. "Now go, before it's too late. We both know that your business will suffer if your name gets linked to mine."

"I'll worry about that when it happens." She made no move toward the door. She didn't want to leave him alone in this gray cell that smelled so strongly of disinfectant and despair.

He looked at her for a minute, and she saw his throat work. Then his jaw hardened. "Get out of here. Just...get out."

"You aren't guilty," she choked. "I know you aren't."

"Hell of a lot of difference that makes. Now *get out*." He turned his back on her, his hands knotted into fists at his sides.

Reluctantly she walked to the door and called for the guard. "I'm leaving for now," she told Luke. "But I'll be back."

He didn't answer, and she left him like that, locked in his own silence.

Before leaving the sheriff's station, Gloria succeeded in learning the details of the charges against Luke. When she returned to her office, she explained what she'd learned to Alice.

"One hundred thousand dollars was deposited in Lockington's personal account. The district attorney has the canceled check, which is allegedly Luke's. Now someone would have to be pretty stupid to use their personal check in such a situation, and we both know Luke is not stupid."

"Difficult," Alice observed dryly, "but not stupid."

"I say someone stole one of his checks, or had some made up to incriminate Luke. This is a frame-up. I know it is."

"Well, his lawyer will take care of it."

Gloria remembered the way Luke had withdrawn from her. "I hope so." But she wasn't going to take a chance on it. Somehow she had to figure out a way to prove his innocence. The question was, how? Jurisprudence and domestic political corruption were out of her sphere of experience.

"You have your class with the ladies tonight. Do you want me to call them and cancel?"

"No. I can't just sit and worry." She enjoyed her time with the Cahill wives—bimbettes, as they'd taken to calling themselves, secretly thumbing their collective nose at the snobbery of others. Their good humor, lack of pretension, and desire to learn made them good company.

She went back into her office and tracked down Josh on the telephone. Gloria told him that she'd been to see Luke, but skirted the more personal details of that meeting. Josh promised to keep her posted on anything that happened.

"I thought you'd want to know that the hearing's been set, which means that Luke should be out on bail by four o' clock tomorrow afternoon."

"Josh, someone should stay with him. He's already been injured once—"

"I saw." Anger seethed through Josh's words.

"He wouldn't let me stay with him," she said, her stomach churning at the memory. "He's trying to protect me. He—" she took a deep breath and plunged "—he said no decent woman is safe with a Cahill."

Josh sighed. "Yeah. That figures."

"*Any* woman would be lucky to be loved by a Cahill."

"I've always thought so." She heard the smile in his voice. Then he grew serious again. "Be patient with him, Gloria. He'd kill me for saying this, but he needs you. You have ... well ... *honor.*"

Honor? How would Josh know a thing like that? She asked him as much.

"I've been talking with Bunnie," he said. "She takes your class," he added, as if he wasn't sure she'd know who he was talking about.

"I know who Bunnie is. She's trying very hard to get her life in order."

"Yeah. I guess the Cahills were poison for her."

Gloria didn't miss his wistful note of regret. "I don't believe she thinks that at all, Josh. Just keep talking with her."

A few hours later, as Gloria was saying goodbye to Wade Anderson in the reception area of Hamilton Consulting, Tiffany and two of her sisters-in-law showed up.

"This is a pleasant surprise," Gloria said as she performed introductions. As the Cahill women politely responded, she took the opportunity to observe their latest fashion transformation. More subtle hair color and makeup and stylish yet flattering clothing served to showcase the women's natural beauty. They'd managed, however, to maintain their love of the dramatic. Gloria smiled. She'd found she was acquiring a taste for bold colors and artistic jewelry. Yes, the so-called Bimbo Brides were something special. Those Cahill men sure could pick 'em.

"We heard about Luke," Tiffany said, "and we came right over. We thought you might, you know, want some company."

"Thanks a lot, ladies," said Alice, who had been working quietly at her computer. "What am I, chopped liver?"

"Oh, we're sorry, Alice," tall, blond Betsy said, instantly contrite. "We didn't mean it that way. It's just that sometimes when a girl—"

"Woman," Tiffany corrected.

"Woman feels really down, it's good to have her friends around. More than one. You know, a little party, sort of."

Alice smiled. "Yes, I know."

"I heard about what happened with Luke Cahill," Wade said. "I guess we should have seen it coming."

Everyone else in the room turned to him. "Why?" they demanded all at once.

"Well," he said, almost apologetically, "maybe it's just because I own the company that has the contract to service the county's computers. I talk with people. The quiet people. The ones who get their work done without drawing notice. The ones who see and hear things because the movers and shakers don't bother to look around. Lockington is corrupt. The man's been feathering his nest with bribe money for years, but Cahill has continually refused to bribe him. In fact, Cahill blew the whistle on him once, but Lockington is so entrenched in Sharlow County politics that his only punishment was embarrassment. Unfortunately, not enough to get him out of office. He hates Cahill's guts, and I imagine that hate quotient has gone up over the Blue Bonnet development.''

"Why?" Gloria asked again.

"Because that's a big development, which would mean big bribes. But so far, Cahill has managed to circumvent Lockington's machinery. Maybe Lockington is making an example. Maybe he's sending a warning to other developers."

Fear for Luke swept through her. "What do you think will happen, Wade?"

Sympathetic brown eyes met hers. "I hear the evidence is pretty damning. Cahill's check. And, of course, the commissioner's word. Unless, by some miracle, Cahill can prove his innocence, he'll go to prison."

Josh called the following morning to tell Gloria that the judge refused to immediately release Luke on bail. After the incident in the lobby of the sheriff's station, Luke had been given a few days' cooling-down time before he would be given a chance for bail. The gnawing, panicked feeling that had vibrated inside her since Luke had sent her from his cell gradually crystallized into hard, uncompromising determination. As soon as she hung up the telephone, she headed out the door on her way to the jail.

Luke refused to see her.

She wanted to tear down the walls that separated them. She wanted to scream at him for not admitting her. She wanted to cry away her breaking heart. Only that diamond-hard core of determination kept her outwardly composed.

Unless, by some miracle, Cahill can prove his innocence, he'll go to prison.

Damn Luke. Damn his pride and his hurt and his bull-headedness. He needed help. He needed the loving support she could give him. Well, by God, he was going to get it. If that angered him, she'd just have to deal with that later. For now, he needed her, and she refused to fail him.

As soon as she got back to the office, she dialed Wade Anderson's number. His secretary got him on the line.

"Gloria, what can I help you with?" he said.

"A miracle, Wade. Here's what I'd like you to do."

Gloria and Wade, Alice and her fiancé, Vern, Josh, Maudie and the Cahill women set up their own information highway. Wade manned the computer and "spoke" to the quiet people he'd mentioned. Alice handled the telephones and maps and generally ran the "war room," which was, in fact, Hamilton Consulting. Vern and his buddies combed every construction site in Sharlow County and talked with the men who worked on them. Maudie conferred with the matriarchs of Tidewater and the smaller towns that populated Sharlow. Gloria and the Cahill wives talked to everyone they could think of. Women, they discovered, were not perceived as threatening. People talked to them. As they talked, Gloria learned how highly Luke was regarded. She also learned that Lockington had, over the years, stepped on a lot of people—people who had become his enemies.

Dirt came sweeping out from under the Sharlow-Tidewater political carpet. But so far, none of it could get Luke out of jail.

Luke sat on his cot and stared at the gray cell wall across from him. He'd tried to get interested in one of the paperbacks that Josh had brought him, but he couldn't concentrate.

He was going crazy in here. He wanted to pound the crap out of Lockington. He wanted his freedom. But mostly, he wanted to gather Gloria in his arms and hold her. She'd come to the station four times in the past two days, asking to see him. Each time, he'd had his jailers send her away. He needed to tell her why, needed to tell her how the media would tar her with the same brush they'd used on his family for years.

She didn't deserve to have her character inspected and ridiculed like that. He wouldn't let it happen to her.

But he missed her. God, how he missed her. The thought that she might believe he didn't want her tore him up inside, but he couldn't risk her reputation. He wouldn't drag her down with him.

"She was here again."

Luke turned to discover the speaker was one of the men in tan who checked on him periodically. "Did you send her away, Joe?"

"Yeah. Just like you told me to." The wiry deputy shook his head as he gazed through the bars. "Think you should let her come see you, though. It breaks a body's heart to see her draw up, all dignified-like. Anyone can see she's hurtin' inside. But she's always so polite. Always thanks me. Asks me to keep you safe." Joe's thin face cracked a small, sad smile. "Guess she saw that bruise on your face." The smile eased away, back into the tanned-leather crevices. "She's a damned fine lady."

"Yeah," Luke said hoarsely. "She's a real lady, all right."

"We have a witness," Tiffany crowed in triumph as soon as she arrived. It was the third of the nightly war councils held in Gloria's living room.

Gloria's head snapped up. She had been dully taking notes—notes that she had jotted for an eternal three days of obtaining no concrete evidence against Lockington. A murmur of hope rippled through the crowd that took up the chairs and couch or sat on the carpet.

"Lockington's secretary," Tiffany continued. "She'd been working a lot of overtime. About a month ago, she overheard Lockington and his buddies. They had a check they'd stolen from Luke. Picked his pocket. The creeps thought it was real funny. Anyway, she heard their plan. The commissioner is out to get Luke for blowing the whistle on him years ago. Lockington's wife left him over that fiasco, though that point was kept out of the papers. Well, one of Lockington's people, at his suggestion, forged Luke's name on this check for one hundred thousand dollars. It was to be deposited to Lockington's personal account by mail, so no one could see who was depositing it. They even planned to drop the envelope in the postbox in the lobby of the Grimble Building."

"Is this woman willing to testify?" Gloria asked, almost afraid to breathe, hope flaming white within her.

"Yes."

"Why didn't she come forward sooner?" Wade asked.

"She was afraid for her job," said Bunnie, who was sitting next to Josh on the floor. Over the last few days, the two of them had become almost inseparable.

"If she's willing to testify, Lockington is had," Josh declared.

Anger churned inside Gloria. Lockington and his cohorts should suffer. She wanted the cop who'd been responsible for Luke's "fall" to suffer. She wanted the corrupt judge to suffer. Because of them, the man she loved more than anyone else in the world had been exposed to ridicule and avid speculation. His good name—a name he'd struggled to protect—had been tarnished. Because of them, Luke had sent her away.

"Has she come forward yet?" she asked.

"I spoke to her just before I got here," Tiffany said glancing at her watch. "She promised she would call the district attorney's office first thing tomorrow morning."

Gloria drew in a long, shaky breath. Dear God, could this mean an end to Luke's ordeal?

By the following afternoon, the news was out—the charges against Luke had been dropped. Faced with a determined witness, Lockington had immediately turned against his coconspirators, loudly claiming his innocence The attorneys were back at work, but this time it looked bad for Lockington. His enemies were uniting for his downfall

Luke didn't call her after he'd been released. He didn' come to see her. It seemed he was determined to keep her ou of his life.

Gloria stood by the telephone in her kitchen for severa minutes before she swallowed and reached out a trembling hand to dial White Oaks. Maudie answered.

"May I speak to Luke?" Gloria asked, vaguely hearing how thin her voice sounded.

"He's not here, dear," Maudie said gently.

Gloria swallowed. "Do you...do you know when he'll be in?"

"He went to the lodge. Said he was going to work on the roof. Personally, I just think he needs some time alone."

Gloria felt as if she were breaking apart, shattering like a stained-glass window. Desperately she tried to hold together for a few minutes longer. "Maudie, may I come over and talk to you? I need...I need to ask some questions. Perhaps it will help me understand."

"What questions?" Maudie asked, her voice warm and sympathetic.

"Why does Luke have such a thing about ladies? About—about bimbos."

"I'm afraid the answers you need must come from Luke, dear. He'll tell you if he chooses. I will say this, he hasn't had an easy life. His mother has a lot to answer for. So does my brother, for that matter. And Barbara Tuttle."

The last name Maudie mentioned rang a distant bell in Gloria's memory. Barbara Tuttle—the waitress?

"Why don't you come over anyway?" Maudie asked. "It doesn't sound as if you should be alone now."

Gloria looked at Hamlet, who regarded her solemnly. With a flutter of wings, he crossed the short distance between his perch and her shoulder. He edged close to her ear and nuzzled it. "Thank you all the same, Maudie. I'm not alone."

After Gloria hung up, she just stood there, stroking Hamlet's soft feathers with the back of her forefinger. "It looks as if it's just you and me again, fella."

Chapter Eleven

Five nights after Luke's release, Gloria heard the roar of an automobile in her driveway. A car door slammed, and a few minutes later, there was an impatient knock at her door. Even before she opened it, she knew who stood on her front porch.

Tall, lean and broad shouldered, Luke Cahill never failed to take her breath away. Tonight, his bright gold hair, dark amber in the porch light, lacked its usual style, looking instead as if he'd shoved his hand through it several times. He wore a midnight blue T-shirt and a gray linen jacket. His indigo jeans hugged his long legs and slim hips like a lover. Her eyes moved lower, down to his favorite Western boots.

"Can I come in?" he asked shortly.

She stepped back to let him pass inside, clinging to an impassive expression, unwilling to let him see how his nearness affected her, how it made her heart pound faster, her breath come harder. "Did you ever get the property for the Children's Fund?" she asked casually, determined to find an impersonal anchor against the storm of hurt and need that raged inside her.

"Yes," he said shortly as he strode through the entrance hall and into her living room. He glanced at Hamlet's empty perch, then at her.

"He's upstairs," she said, answering his unspoken question. "I was just getting ready to go to bed." She felt cold and panicky inside.

Luke faced her. His azure gaze pierced her like a laser. "Why did you ask my aunt about my feelings, about my past?" he demanded. "I'm the one who proposed to you. Not her. If you have questions, you can damn well ask them of me."

"You were unavailable." Gloria lifted her chin. "Besides, I thought that wouldn't matter to you anymore."

He stared at her. Color rose in his high, classic cheekbones. "Not matter anymore? Well, that's a damned foolish thing to think."

"You refused to see me!" she cried. "Then, when you finally got out, you left and didn't even call me to say you were all right."

"I was trying to protect you! And afterward... I needed time to think. I'm sorry I didn't call you. But how could you doubt me like this? Gloria. I asked you to marry me. That should mean *something*."

She met his gaze directly and was shaken to see hurt mingled with the anger. A knot clenched in her gut. "I didn't think that still applied," she said.

He drove his hand through his hair. "You thought I'd taken back my proposal of marriage?"

"What was I supposed to think? You all but threw me out of your cell. You refused to see me again. And then you took off as soon as you were released without so much as a phone call to me."

"But that doesn't mean I don't want to marry you," he insisted.

"Does it mean I've passed your tests?"

Luke went absolutely still.

"Did I score well?" she persisted, driven by her own anger, her own hurt. "When you rang the bell, did I perform to your satisfaction?"

He turned away, every line in his graceful body tense. "It wasn't like that."

"No?" she snapped.

He spun around to face her again. "*No.* I didn't like doing it, making tests to see—" He broke off, swearing vehemently beneath his breath. "I hated it! God, I felt lower than a snake. But I had to see. I had to. . . to make sure."

She moved closer to him, touched by his deep distress, which vibrated through the room. "Sure of what?"

He looked away, his dark gold eyebrows drawn down, his sensual mouth forming a flat line. Gloria studied his beloved face, remembering how he could make her feel. Sexy. Desired. With him, she seemed to lose her dullness. With Luke, she came alive.

"Sure of what?" she repeated. She took a step toward him when he didn't answer. "That I wasn't like your mother?" she asked softly. "Like Barbara Tuttle?"

His head snapped around, and she felt seared by his eyes. "What do you know about my mother? About Barbara?"

Gloria closed the distance between them. She dared to lay her palm against his cheek, half-afraid he might pull away. "Little. Too little. Maudie said you'd tell me if you chose."

He looked at her for a long moment. It occurred to her that he might refuse, that he might turn and walk out the door, out of her life, and suddenly that thought frightened her.

She loved him.

He was like no man she'd ever known before. Caring, teasing, hard and crazy by turns. Maybe he was crazy for wanting to marry her, she thought. Maybe she was crazy for wanting him. But want him she did.

"My mother didn't much like Josh and me," he said slowly, his voice shadowed with remembered pain. "She said we'd ruined her figure—*I'd* ruined her figure. She used to shout at me about it. Call me a damn brat. Tell me that I was going to be as bad as my old man, knocking up some poor woman and getting her fat and ugly so no other man would want her."

Gloria stared at him in horrified disbelief. How could a woman treat her child so cruelly?

"She liked men." Luke's beautiful mouth drew down. "At first, she made excuses to my father. A flat tire. A sick friend. But word always gets around in a small town. Dad learned that she'd been hanging out in bars. He learned she'd slept with other men. No, not slept with them. That's too nice a term. I was in my room when I heard her and Dad screaming at each other. I guess it was the night he first found out."

"How...how old were you?"

"Seven. I was seven. And she called my father the worst, most disgusting names. Said he'd loaded her down with two house apes and never wanted her to have any fun. I couldn't hear what he said—his voice was too low. But I heard what she said clear enough. She shouted that she wasn't his damn broodmare, that he'd gotten all the brats off her he was going to. She'd gotten fixed."

Gloria felt numbed by the hateful callousness of Luke's mother. "Did Josh hear?"

Luke shook his head. Distractedly he picked up a small porcelain rose from a table and examined it. "No. He was asleep."

He continued to stare at the rose for a minute, then set it back down. "Dad locked himself in the study and got falling-down drunk. Mom left and didn't come back for days."

"Who took care of you and Josh?"

"The cook. She took us home with her. There was no one around to miss us." A ghost of a smile played around the corners of his lips. "Riva had five kids of her own. She needed two more like she needed a hole in the head, but I never heard a word of complaint from anyone in her family. God, I loved going over there."

"Did you go often?"

His gaze dropped to the carpet. He nodded. "Yeah. Things pretty much fell apart at home. Mom catted around and slept with just about any man who could perform—the lower and trashier, the better—and Dad came home from the office and headed straight for the bottle." Luke looked out the window into the dark. In the distance, a dog barked. "Every so often, she'd come to my school, always lookin' like a cheap streetwalker. She'd take Josh and me out of class, then drive us around town. She never said anything, never talked to us. One time, she took us to a bar. I remember it stank. It was so dark inside you could fall over your own feet. Mom got . . . distracted. She must have forgotten about us and gone off with one of her boyfriends." He shrugged one shoulder. "The cops picked us up and took us down to the station. Maudie came to pick us up. After that, we saw a lot more of Maudie. When her husband died, she moved to White Oaks. Dad went to a treatment center. When he came back, he divorced Mom and eventually took out a restraining order against her. I was in high school by then."

Gloria felt ill with disgust at Lydia Cahill and at the way Daniel Cahill had abdicated his responsibilities to his sons.

"My mother was, and is, a tramp of the first order," Luke said flatly.

Gloria had seen Lydia—the sex-kitten clothing, the heavy makeup. It was all too clear to her where Luke had gotten his aversion to bimbos. She wanted to tell him that the heavy-handed use of cosmetics and the choice of sexy clothing didn't necessarily mean that a woman had the morals of an alley cat, or worse, his mother. But Luke's terrible experiences had left their mark.

"And Barbara Tuttle?" Gloria asked softly. "At the barbecue, someone said she worked as a waitress at a . . . nudie place. Did you stop dating her because of it?"

Luke laughed, a short, sharp, hollow sound. "Are you kidding? I was crazy about Barbara. Yeah, she was a waitress in a strip joint off the old highway. She told me she was a college student, working to raise the money for her tuition. I wanted to marry her as soon as I finished at the university." He made a harsh noise in his throat. "God, what a sap I was. I broke my back working an extra job so I could buy her an engagement ring. We even set a date for the wedding."

He fell silent for several minutes.

"What happened?" Gloria prompted, needing to know, to learn why Luke carried with him such a distrust.

He shoved his hands into his jeans pockets. "I dropped by unexpected at the place where she worked. She wasn't in the bar area. She was upstairs—with a man. When I confronted her, she confessed she'd been sleeping around for money." His mouth twisted and he turned away from Gloria to stare out the dark window. "I try not to be so stupid these days."

She grieved for the boy who'd survived a tormented childhood, only to have his little remaining innocence harshly stripped away by someone he'd cared for, someone he'd trusted. Looking at him now, this beautiful man who stood so stiffly by her window, Gloria's throat tightened.

He deserved so much better than he'd received. Yet if she hadn't pushed the point, she would never have known why he'd tested her. Slowly she walked across the room to him. Her pushing had opened old wounds for him. Now she must tell him her reason for doing so.

She laid her hand gently on his shoulder. "You hurt me, Luke, and I needed to know why."

He turned his head. His eyes went first to her hand, then to her face. His thick, gilded lashes remained lowered just enough to protect himself from her glimpsing what might be revealed. "I never meant to hurt you." Like wood smoke, his emotions drifted through his deep drawl, touching his words with more than spoken meaning.

"How did you think I'd feel?" Her question bore no anger.

"I hoped you'd never find out about the tests."

Gloria's lips curved up faintly. "Would you want a woman so dense she couldn't guess what you were doing?"

He lifted his lashes. In his vivid blue eyes, she recognized guarded hope. "No, I suppose not."

"Is it so important to you whether I'm a lady or not?"

The tender corners of his mouth tightened. "You are a lady. Once, that was important to me."

Her heart contracted with fear. "Once?" Had he changed his mind? Decided she wasn't worth the trouble?

"Somehow..." He breathed in deeply. "Somehow that doesn't matter to me anymore."

Gloria swallowed hard against the lump that expanded in her throat.

"You're the only thing that matters to me, Gloria. *You.* Not the fact that you're a lady. Not your cooking or your decorating. You." His eyes revealed what she'd hoped to find. "I love you."

She tried to blink back warm tears, then abandoned the effort. "Oh, Luke."

He gathered her into his arms and rocked her as she wept. He tucked her head into the warm curve of his throat and murmured softly, his sweet assurances rumbling in his chest, vibrating through her skin, into her heart.

She sniffled. "I was afraid you only wanted me because I'm a good hostess." And despite his words, a fragment of concern remained.

He moved away from her just enough to look into her face. "Whatever gave you that idea?"

Her mouth trembled. "It's happened before."

He scowled. "It has?"

She nodded.

He studied her a moment, then, with a long sigh, tucked her back against him. "It seems you know a lot of stupid people, sweetheart."

They stood silent for a moment. Gloria took comfort in the steady sound of his heartbeat.

"After my mother died," she said, "I learned to be a hostess. Oh, not at first. I was much too young to oversee the dinners or the entertainment arrangements. But I was eager to learn." Her mouth tightened with old bitterness. "Oh, I was eager. You see, that was the only time I ever really saw my father. The only time he noticed my existence. So by the time I was eighteen, I was his official hostess."

Luke smoothed his fingers through her hair. "You've never told me how your mother died."

"A sniper shot her." New tears welled up. New tears for an old feeling of futility and loss and a despairing sense of waste. "We were hurrying to the car to go to the plane that would lift the last of the embassy personnel out of the country." The memory of the *pop* of rifle fire, of the way her mother's body had jerked, of the small, surprised exclamation that had burst from her mother's lips still haunted Gloria. Widened blue eyes, filled with confusion one instant, empty and glazing the next. Gloria had looked into them as she'd knelt on the ground, terrified, calling to her mother to return. Seconds later, she'd been surrounded by armed marines. One of them had placed the first two fingers of one hand on her mother's neck and peered into the staring eyes. Looking up at his superior, he gave one quick, negative shake of his head, then gently brushed his hand over the still face. When his hand came away, the eyes were closed. The next thing Gloria remembered was sitting numbly on the bench of the transport plane with Alice's arms around her.

"I came back to Texas to attend the university. That's where my mother's family was. They're all gone now, though. There weren't many of them." She'd had little time with her grandparents before first one, and then the other had passed away. The few others had seemed content to remain strangers. "I met Charles at school. He was from a small farm in West Texas and was working his way through. He was filled with fire and determination to make a better life for himself. He was handsome and charming, and he told me that he needed me." She sighed. "I was lonely and foolish enough to believe him. But he never needed me. He never even wanted me. What he wanted was what I knew. He wanted a wife who could teach him to be a gentleman. A wife who could impress his associates and superiors with her skills as a hostess or conversationalist. He wanted a wife who would be an asset to him while he climbed to the top." Would she ever be free of the rejection and betrayal she'd felt since she'd discovered Charles with Suzette? "When he reached the top, he wanted his secretary."

Luke enfolded her more firmly in the warm sanctuary of his arms. He kissed the top of her head. "He deserves his secretary."

"I'm sure he's very happy with his choice," she said miserably. She knew she'd never really loved Charles, certainly not as she loved Luke, but she had trusted him. She'd thought that in this violent, miraculous, ruthless world, they had been a team. And she'd been wrong. So very wrong.

"Well," Luke said, "he's paying through the nose to build her a big, gaudy house. Her shopping sprees have cost him a fortune. And she's already betrayed him."

Gloria lifted her head. "Suzette's betrayed him?"

Luke nodded. She read the glint of satisfaction in his eyes. "She's sleeping with his boss, the CEO. Seems she's aiming higher than dear old Charles."

"How do you know this?"

"I set a detective on them. I don't like what they did to you. And someday, when just the right opportunity arises, I'm going to make them pay." His words were casually spoken, but she heard the steel in them.

"No, Luke," she said, pleased by his willingness to throw down his gauntlet on her behalf. "They're working on their own misery."

"They'll never be miserable enough to satisfy me," he muttered, and she glowed inside.

After a moment, he said, "You haven't given me your answer."

Gloria looked up at him in question.

"Will you be my wife?"

She searched his face as if she could find the answer there. "I think we need time."

His eyebrows lowered. "Time for what?"

"To get to know each other better."

"Better?" he growled. "Don't you mean time to find faults?"

Despite the uncertainty that quivered inside her stomach, the fear that she was casting aside a golden chance for happiness, she gave no ground. Instead, she widened her eyes in feigned surprise. "Are there faults to find? Goodness, who would have guessed!"

"What you see is what you get."

She reached up to trace with her fingertips the stubborn line of his beautiful mouth. "Not always, my love. I know your experience has shown you differently, but what you see is *not* always what you get. Charles presented the image of an aw-shucks, good-hearted, down-home cowboy. But beneath that sweet exterior lurked a ruthless shark. How do you know I'm not just another Charles, looking for an easier ride to the top?"

Luke kissed her fingers, then firmly wrapped his hand around them. He pressed them against his chest. "Feel that?" he asked.

Through the fabric of his shirt and the warmth of his skin, she felt the steady, rhythmic beat. She nodded. "Your heart."

His eyes never left hers. "That's right. You have an important place in there. The most important place a woman can hold in a man's heart. As long as mine continues to beat, I'll love you, Gloria. If you're nervous, I understand, but that doesn't change the way I feel."

She was nervous. Although she no longer feared that he wanted her because he needed a socially skilled wife, she knew that life with Luke would not be a glassy sea. He remained unpredictable enough to throw her a high wave every now and then. Maybe that was part of what made her feel so alive when she was with him. Maybe it was the way he made her feel sexy and desirable. She couldn't say for certain. She only knew for sure that sometimes hearts formed bonds of their own that defied logic or length of acquaintance.

The power of what she felt for Luke far outstripped any feelings she'd ever had for Charles—or any other man. It was as if she'd been born with only half a soul. In Luke, she'd discovered the other half. Now, with little more than a month together, she found the thought of life without him unbearable.

"I love you," she said. "I'll always love you."

"Then marry me." He pressed persuasive kisses to her mouth, her cheeks, her temple. "Marry me and I'll make love to you every day and every night—"

"Hot, passionate love?"

"Hotter and more passionate than you've ever imagined."

She smiled as her heart soared with fierce joy. "I don't know, Luke Cahill. I've had some pretty torrid dreams about you."

He grinned, obviously pleased. "You have?"

Gloria laughed. "Yes. Oh, the things I could tell you about those dreams."

"Then marry me and show me what you dreamed."

She lifted her face to him. She hoped their children all had summer blue eyes. "I guess I'll have to," she said. "It will take a lifetime to get it all right."

Epilogue

The second floor of White Oaks was a flurry of giggles and whispers, and a rainbow of lace and petticoats. Below, on the first floor, garlands of ivy and roses decorated the entry hall and festooned the living room, where vases of freshly cut flowers scented the room and cream-colored, padded folding chairs accommodated the wedding guests. Gloria knew that even now Alice and Maudie were greeting those very guests, and that four of Luke's younger cousins were escorting them to their seats.

It would be a rather unusual wedding, Gloria thought with a smile. Few brides had ever had twenty-five matrons of honor. Josh, of course, was Luke's best man, as Luke would be his next month when Bunnie and Josh remarried. Bubba was ring bearer, and Poppy the prettiest little flower girl in the history of Texas.

Gloria would have been satisfied with a small, quiet wedding, but Luke and his family wanted none of that. This was a momentous day and they felt that it should be celebrated with a certain pomp.

"Oh, no, Gloria darlin'!" Bunnie exclaimed, gorgeous in fuchsia lace. "You can't wear such a pale lipstick. It's just not flattering."

Immediately, six other Cahill wives gathered around to study Gloria's makeup and offer their advice.

"She's right, sugar," Betsy said. "Your coloring is much too vivid for that pale little ol' pink. Here—" she handed Gloria a tube of deep pink-plum lipstick "—try this."

Standing in front of the cheval mirror, attired in her silver gray satin-and-lace wedding dress, a pale, frothy veil forming a halo around her face, Gloria applied the brighter lipstick, aware of the scrutiny of her friends.

"There now, that's much better, don't you think?" Bunnie asked, and received a murmur of assent from all the women.

Gloria had to agree. The color was much more becoming.

"No, no, no!" Hamlet declared, which regained him the laughter and attention he'd been receiving all afternoon.

There was a brief knock on the bedroom door, then it opened. In strode Luke, breathtakingly handsome in his tuxedo. He gazed at Gloria for a full minute, his handsome face alight with a smile that had the power to melt her knees.

"You're beautiful," he said quietly, taking her hands in his. He lifted them to his lips and kissed her fingers. Gloria joyfully lost herself in his blue gaze.

"Luke, you devil," admonished Marcy, whose dress was a soft pink lace that complemented her red hair, "you know you're not supposed to see the bride before the wedding."

"By tradition," Luke said, grinning, "but then, there are a lot of traditions that have gotten a new spin with this wedding." Then, to Gloria's surprise, he sobered. "I came to say something to you ladies," he said, his eyes scanning the faces of her matrons of honor. The room grew silent.

"First of all," he said, "I want to say thank you for helping to clear my name of Lockington's accusation."

"It's been three months since you got out of jail," Bunnie remarked. "You've been saying thank you to us ever since."

"And I may continue to say it for years to come. But that's not all I want to say." He glanced at Gloria, then looked back at the other women. "I was wrong. For years I've been critical and unbearable and wrong. I hope you will find it in your hearts to forgive me."

For seconds, the dropping of a pin would have sounded like a crash.

"Welcome!" Hamlet declared, pattering from side to side on his open perch. "Welcome!"

Bunnie went up to Luke and gave him a quick, shy kiss on his cheek. "I hope I speak for all of us when I say what's past is forgotten. Today begins a new start." The voices of the other Cahill wives joined in her sentiment. Smiles wreathed beautiful faces.

"Thank you," he said. "I'll see you all downstairs in—" he glanced at his watch "—ten minutes."

After he left, Gloria opened a container the size of a small hatbox. Inside were twenty-five small, wrapped jeweler's boxes. "Luke and I want you to have these on this special day." She smiled. "Luke insisted on picking them out." She went through the room and out into the hall, making certain each woman received her gift.

Tiffany was the first to open hers. "Oh!" There, on black velvet, lay an exquisite golden heart pendant. In the center of the heart, raised in silver, was a graceful *C*.

Minutes later, when the matrons of honor had assembled near the stairs, everyone wore her pendant.

The pianist struck up the opening chords of the Purcell processional and Gloria began her walk down the center aisle in the living room on the arm of Vern, Alice's husband of two months. She carried the bouquet of wildflowers that her matrons of honor had bought to save her from her own more ordinary choice of rosebuds and baby's breath.

As she passed Alice, Gloria saw her foster mother's eyes glistening with happy tears, and she had to blink rapidly to keep her own at bay.

Finally, Vern delivered her into Luke's keeping, and the minister began the ceremony to sanctify her bond with Luke.

She had traveled a long way from those small embassies in war-torn countries and from that darkened twentieth-floor office in a Houston business building. The journey had been as much of the heart as of distance. It had been rocky and full of detours. But now, as Gloria looked up to meet Luke's smiling gaze, she knew that at last she'd reached her destination. With Luke she would share her life. With Luke she would raise their children. In Luke, her heart had found home.

* * * * *

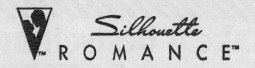

COMING NEXT MONTH

#1108 THE DAD NEXT DOOR—Kasey Michaels
Fabulous Fathers
Quinn Patrick moved in only to find trouble next door—in the
form of lovely neighbor Maddie Pemberton and her son, Dillon.
Was this confirmed bachelor about to end up with a ready-
made family?

#1109 TEMPORARILY HERS—Susan Meier
Bundles of Joy
Katherine Whitman was determined to win custody of her
nephew Jason—even if it meant a temporary marriage to playboy
Alex Cane. Then Katherine found herself falling for her new
"husband" and facing permanent heartache.

#1110 STAND-IN HUSBAND—Anne Peters
Pavel Mallik remembered nothing. All he knew was that the
lovely Marie Cooper had saved his life. Now he had the chance
to rescue her reputation by making her his wife!

#1111 STORYBOOK COWBOY—Pat Montana
Jo McPherson didn't trust Trey Covington. The handsome cowboy
brought back too many memories. Jo tried to resist his charm, but
Trey had his ways of making her forget the past…and dream about
the future.

#1112 FAMILY TIES—Dani Criss
Single mother Laine Sullivan knew Drew Casteel was commitment
shy. It would be smarter to steer clear of the handsome bachelor. But
Drew was hard to resist. Soon Laine had to decide whether or not to
risk her heart….

#1113 HONEYMOON SUITE—Linda Lewis
Premiere
Miranda St. James had always been pursued for her celebrity
connections. So when Stuart Winslow began to woo her, Miranda
kept her identity a secret. But Stuart had secrets of his own!

Take 4 bestselling love stories FREE

Plus get a FREE surprise gift!

Special Limited-time Offer

Mail to Silhouette Reader Service™

3010 Walden Avenue
P.O. Box 1867
Buffalo, N.Y. 14269-1867

YES! Please send me 4 free Silhouette Romance™ novels and my free surprise gift. Then send me 6 brand-new novels every month, which I will receive months before they appear in bookstores. Bill me at the low price of $2.19 each plus 25¢ delivery and applicable sales tax, if any.* That's the complete price and a savings of over 10% off the cover prices—quite a bargain! I understand that accepting the books and gift places me under no obligation ever to buy any books. I can always return a shipment and cancel at any time. Even if I never buy another book from Silhouette, the 4 free books and the surprise gift are mine to keep forever.

215 BPA ANRP

Name	(PLEASE PRINT)	
Address	Apt. No.	
City	State	Zip

This offer is limited to one order per household and not valid to present Silhouette Romance™ subscribers. *Terms and prices are subject to change without notice. Sales tax applicable in N.Y.

USROM-295

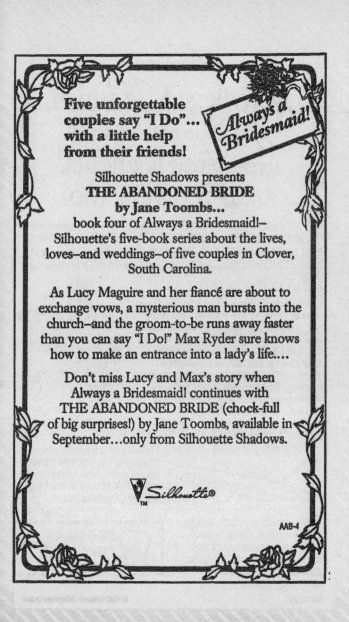

Five unforgettable couples say "I Do"... with a little help from their friends!

Always a Bridesmaid!

Silhouette Shadows presents
THE ABANDONED BRIDE
by Jane Toombs...
book four of Always a Bridesmaid!–
Silhouette's five-book series about the lives,
loves–and weddings–of five couples in Clover,
South Carolina.

As Lucy Maguire and her fiancé are about to
exchange vows, a mysterious man bursts into the
church–and the groom-to-be runs away faster
than you can say "I Do!" Max Ryder sure knows
how to make an entrance into a lady's life....

Don't miss Lucy and Max's story when
Always a Bridesmaid! continues with
THE ABANDONED BRIDE (chock-full
of big surprises!) by Jane Toombs, available in
September...only from Silhouette Shadows.

Silhouette®
TM

AAB-4

Become a Privileged Woman,
You'll be entitled to all these *Free Benefits*. And *Free Gifts*, too.

To thank you for buying our books, we've designed an exclusive FREE program called *PAGES & PRIVILEGES™*. You can enroll with just one Proof of Purchase, and get the kind of luxuries that, until now, you could only read about.

BIG HOTEL DISCOUNTS

A privileged woman stays in the finest hotels. And so can you—at up to 60% off! Imagine standing in a hotel check-in line and watching as the guest in front of you pays $150 for the same room that's only costing you $60. Your *Pages & Privileges* discounts are good at Sheraton, Marriott, Best Western, Hyatt and thousands of other fine hotels all over the U.S., Canada and Europe.

FREE DISCOUNT TRAVEL SERVICE

A privileged woman is always jetting to romantic places. When <u>you</u> fly, just make one phone call for the lowest published airfare at time of booking— <u>or double the difference back!</u>

PLUS—you'll get a $25 voucher to use the first time you book a flight AND <u>5% cash back on every ticket you buy thereafter through the travel service!</u>